# THE PHANTOM MENACE™

**STAR WARS REBEL FORCE**

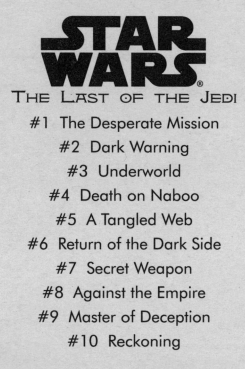

**STAR WARS THE LAST OF THE JEDI**

# EPISODE I

## THE PHANTOM MENACE™

Patricia C. Wrede

Based on the screenplay and story
by George Lucas

## SCHOLASTIC INC.

New York  Toronto  London  Auckland  Sydney
Mexico City  New Delhi  Hong Kong  Buenos Aires

ISBN-13: 978-0-590-01089-4
ISBN-10: 0-590-01089-1

Cover photo montage by Paul Colin. Book design by Madalina Stefan.

23 22 21 20 19 18 17                                     14 15 16 17/0

Printed in the U.S.A.

First Scholastic printing, June 1999

**A** *long time ago in a galaxy far, far away . . .*

Before the Rebel Alliance fought its way to freedom; before the Jedi Knights all but vanished from the known worlds; before the Empire was founded to expand like a cancer across the stars — before any of these things occurred, the Galactic Republic ruled much of the galaxy.

It was a time of peace, watched over by the Jedi Knights and Masters. But the Jedi were guardians only, using their amazing fighting skills to defend justice. They were the Republic's peacemakers; its rulers were the members of the Galactic Senate. Thousands of delegates, representing every planet in the Republic, met regularly in the great Senate chambers on the central world of Coruscant. There they wrote the laws of the Republic and settled the disputes that sometimes arose between planets.

Over the centuries, many problems came before

the Senate. At first, the dispute over taxing trade routes seemed no different from all the others. The Trade Federation — an organization of merchants so powerful that they had a representative in the Galactic Senate, just as if they were a planet — wanted more control in the outlying star systems. The outlying planets objected. The debate dragged on and on.

Finally the Trade Federation lost patience, and took more drastic action. They chose the small, watery world of Naboo and blockaded it, surrounding it with battleships so that no spaceships could land or take off from the planet. They hoped that the young Queen of Naboo would agree quickly to their demands. Then they could use Naboo as an example to persuade or force other planets to do the same.

But the young Queen did not give in. Tension in the Senate grew worse. Worried that the Trade Federation's blockade might lead to open war, the Supreme Chancellor of the Galactic Senate asked the Jedi for help. Soon, two Jedi ambassadors were on their way to Naboo to settle the conflict. They expected their mission to be short and simple. . . .

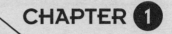

The Galactic Republic's cruiser dropped out of hyperspace at last, giving Qui-Gon Jinn his first look at Naboo — or rather, at the menacing cloud of Trade Federation battleships that surrounded it. Like fat white maggots, they spread through space, blocking all access to the planet. Qui-Gon was not impressed. In the decades he had been a Jedi Knight, he had seen many battleships. The ships were unimportant; what mattered were the beings they carried.

The view screen lit. Leaning forward, Qui-Gon peered over the cruiser captain's shoulder. The screen showed a Neimoidian with grayish-tan skin and dull orange eyes, wearing a three-pronged headdress. *One of the Trade Federation's viceroys. Does he greet all incoming ships personally, or only ambassadors?* Qui-Gon wondered. "Captain," he said aloud. "Tell them we wish to board at once."

"Yes, sir." The captain looked back at her view

screen. "With all due respect for the Trade Federation, the ambassadors for the Supreme Chancellor wish to board immediately," she told the Neimoidian.

"Yes, yes, of course," the viceroy replied. "Ah, as you know, our blockade is legal, perfectly legal. We'll be happy to receive the ambassadors. . . ." The view screen went black.

The main Trade Federation battleship loomed ahead. Qui-Gon closed his eyes, carefully testing the feel of the Force. *The ship carries mainly Neimoidians. And they're nervous.* About what he had expected. And yet . . . something else hovered ominously on the edge of his perception, something he could not quite identify.

The impression faded as the cruiser settled to the floor of the battleship's docking bay. Qui-Gon opened his eyes. Whatever he had sensed, it was gone. Now he had more immediate duties to attend to.

Rising, Qui-Gon motioned to Obi-Wan. The younger Jedi's face was stern, as befitted an important mission, and Qui-Gon sighed. Not for the first time, he wondered what Master Yoda had been thinking all those years ago, when he brought Qui-Gon and Obi-Wan Kenobi together as Master and Padawan apprentice. Obi-Wan Kenobi had great skill, no question of that, but sometimes he was so . . . intense.

Qui-Gon smiled slightly. Master Yoda always saw farther than anyone else. Perhaps he had thought that an earnest young apprentice would be as good for Qui-Gon as Qui-Gon would be for the apprentice. It would be like Yoda to balance Obi-Wan's headstrong nature and by-the-book methods against Qui-Gon's patience and unconventional ways. He would have to ask Yoda about it, after Obi-Wan passed the trials and became a full Jedi Knight. *That will be soon*, Qui-Gon thought — though he hadn't said anything about it to Obi-Wan yet.

As he came down the exit ramp, Qui-Gon saw a protocol droid waiting below. Obi-Wan's eyebrows rose, and he gave Qui-Gon a quick, questioning look. Qui-Gon nodded in reassurance. Neimoidians were a nervous race, happiest doing business at a distance. They were probably still trying to get up the courage to face the ambassadors in person.

The droid led them to a large room equipped with a round conference table. One entire wall was made of windows, providing a spectacular view of the planet Naboo . . . and the fleet of battleships surrounding it. *Not the best background for peace talks*, Qui-Gon thought.

"I hope your honored sirs will be most comfortable here," the protocol droid said. "My master will be with you shortly." Bowing, it left.

Obi-Wan put back the hood of his cloak, revealing

short dark hair with a single thin braid dangling over one shoulder. He was shorter than Qui-Gon, and clean shaven. Qui-Gon wore his graying hair long, and sported a small, neat beard. Only their clothing was similar; both wore the dark, hooded cloaks and cream-colored tunics of the Jedi order.

Obi-Wan stared out the window at the battle fleet. "I have a bad feeling about this," he said finally.

"I don't sense anything," Qui-Gon said. The faint disturbance he had felt earlier had vanished completely. But though Obi-Wan was only twenty-five and not yet a full Jedi Knight, he had great sensitivity to the Force. Qui-Gon had learned to respect his apprentice's instincts. *Some new problem, then?*

"It's not about the mission, Master," Obi-Wan said quickly. "It's something elsewhere. Elusive . . ."

"Don't center on your anxiety, Obi-Wan," Qui-Gon warned. "Keep your concentration here and now, where it belongs."

"Master Yoda says I should be mindful of the future."

"But not at the expense of the moment," Qui-Gon said gently. "Be mindful of the living Force, my young Padawan."

Obi-Wan's preoccupied expression held a moment longer. Then he nodded. "Yes, Master."

The two men stood silent, looking out at the fleet. After a time, Obi-Wan said, "How do you think this trade viceroy will deal with the Chancellor's demands?"

"These Federation types are cowards," Qui-Gon said. "The negotiations will be short." But as he spoke, he wondered. The trade viceroy was taking a long time to arrive, even for a Neimoidian. He shook his head. Staring at the Trade Federation's fleet disturbed his thoughts. Deliberately, he turned away. Taking a seat at the table, he began to calm his mind.

After a moment, Obi-Wan joined him. "Is it in their nature to make us wait this long?" he asked, voicing Qui-Gon's own unease.

"No," Qui-Gon said. He paused, concentrating. "I sense an unusual amount of fear for something as trivial as this trade dispute."

Nute Gunray, the Trade Federation viceroy, had been nervous since the blockade began. He had been frightened ever since the Republic cruiser entered the Naboo star system. Now, standing on the bridge of his battleship and facing the communication hologram of Darth Sidious, he was quite frankly terrified.

*Darth Sidious frightens everyone*, thought Nute, but it was small comfort. The Sith Lord was a shadowy, evil figure. Even though the Trade Federation had followed him loyally, he always wore a hooded cloak that hid most of his face from his allies. *Mysterious . . . and powerful*, Nute reminded himself. Somehow the thought was not as reassuring as he had intended it to be.

Beside him, Daultay Dofine stammered objections and explanations to the Sith Lord's hologram. "The ambassadors are Jedi!" Dofine finished. "We dare not go against them."

The holographic image of Sidious shifted. "You seem more worried about these Jedi than you are about me, Dofine," came the soft, menacing voice. "I am amused."

Dofine seemed to shrink. Sidious turned. "Viceroy!"

Nute's skull ridges went cold, and he had to force himself to step forward. "Yes, my lord?"

"I don't want that stunted slime in my sight again," Sidious said. "Do you understand?"

"Yes, my lord," Nute said, and glared at Dofine until he ran off the bridge.

"This turn of events is unfortunate." Darth Sidious went on as if nothing had happened. "We must accelerate our plans. Begin landing your troops."

Nute stared, completely taken aback. Thousands of battle droids stood ready in the holds of his battleships, but he hadn't expected to actually have to *use* them. "Ahh, my lord . . . is that legal?" Nute asked tentatively.

"I will make it legal," the hooded figure said flatly.

Nute shivered. Sidious' tone left no room for doubts or questions. *If he can make an invasion legal, what else is he capable of?*

"And the Jedi?" Nute asked.

"The Chancellor should never have brought them into this," Sidious said. "Kill them immediately."

"Y-yes, my lord. As you wish," Nute stammered automatically. *Oh, no. Even he can't make that legal.* He stared at the dark figure in the hooded cloak and swallowed hard. *But if I refuse, he'll be angry. And facing Darth Sidious is terrible enough when he's pleased. . . .*

The figure chuckled, as if Sidious knew what Nute had been thinking. The hologram winked out. Nute took a deep breath of relief, then turned to the ship's interior controls. A touch of a button switched the main screen to a view of the docking bay where the Republic cruiser sat. Another button brought a gun to bear on the cruiser. Nute barely hesitated before he pushed the button down. The gun fired, and the Republic cruiser exploded.

"That was easy enough," Nute muttered to himself. "Now for the Jedi . . ."

Qui-Gon felt the deaths of the cruiser's crew at once. Immediately, he sprang to his feet, lightsaber in hand. He noted with approval that Obi-Wan also sensed the disturbance in the Force and reacted quickly. Together they scanned the room, weapons ready. No threat appeared, only the protocol droid dithering over its spilled drinks.

Qui-Gon nodded at Obi-Wan, and they turned off their lightsabers. The hum of the weapons died. In the quiet, Qui-Gon heard a faint hissing.

"Gas!" he called to Obi-Wan. He took a deep breath and held it. They would have to fight their way out quickly, or be overcome.

# CHAPTER 2

The holocam in the conference room showed only a thick green cloud. Nute Gunray studied the picture carefully. *The Jedi must be dead by now*, he thought. He switched to a view of the hallway outside the room, where a crowd of skeletal battle droids waited. "Go in and blast what's left of them," he ordered.

The droids readied their weapons. One of them opened the door, and the deadly gas billowed out. Nute tensed, seeing movement in the cloud, but it was only the protocol droid. *The Jedi are dead*, he thought with satisfaction. He reached to shut off the screen.

Two humming bars of light, one green and one blue, swept out of the fog. They passed through the nearest battle droids without pausing. The droids collapsed, cut in half. Alarms began to sound.

Nute leaned forward, trying to make sense of the

confused images. "What in blazes is going on down there?"

"Have you ever encountered a Jedi Knight before, sir?" asked his lieutenant, Rune Haako.

"Not exactly," Nute said. "But I don't —" A screen lit up, showing a string of corridors in red. *They're heading for the bridge!* "Seal the doors!" he shouted.

"That won't be enough, sir," Rune said almost sadly as the doors slammed shut. "That won't be nearly enough."

Qui-Gon's lightsaber sliced through a pair of battle droids. They collapsed in a shower of sparks. The door to the bridge was just ahead. As he parried a shot from another droid, he felt a surge in the Force. An instant later, a group of battle droids flew against the wall and collapsed in a tangle. Qui-Gon nodded approval. His apprentice was making good use of his skills.

He reached the bridge door and began to cut through it, trusting Obi-Wan to hold off any new battle droids. Almost at once, he felt a rush of fear from the room beyond. Then, with a loud rumble, a series of blast doors slammed, sealing the bridge even tighter.

Qui-Gon shook his head, almost amused. Blast doors could not keep out a Jedi. Shifting his grip on his lightsaber, he stabbed at the door. The laser melted the metal rapidly. It would not be long now.

Suddenly, he sensed a change close by. It took only a moment's concentration to find the source. "Destroyer droids!" he said to Obi-Wan, turning away from the blast door.

"Offhand, I'd say this mission is past the negotiation stage," Obi-Wan replied.

*I suppose it's better to have a sense of humor that only shows up in the middle of a battle than to have no sense of humor at all,* Qui-Gon thought.

The two men sprinted down the hall and took cover in a pair of service niches. An instant later, the destroyer droids appeared at the end of the hall. The droids marched past, firing steadily at the smoke-filled area in front of the bridge doors. As soon as they went by, Qui-Gon nodded at Obi-Wan. The two men stepped back into the hall, behind the droids.

One of the destroyer droids seemed to realize something was wrong. "Switch to bio," it commanded. "There they are!"

The droids began firing again, this time in the right direction. Qui-Gon and Obi-Wan used their lightsabers to send the shots back at the droids. But just before each shot struck, a bubble of energy appeared around its target, protecting the droids from damage.

"They have shield generators!" Obi-Wan said.

"It's a standoff," Qui-Gon replied. "Let's go." He and Obi-Wan had no hope of breaking into the bridge now, not with that kind of reinforcement. They'd have to find another way.

In the marble-walled throne room of the palace of Naboo, the Governing Council had assembled at last. Queen Amidala sat on the throne, watching them. The crisis with the Trade Federation had brought the governors from every city of Naboo here, to show their support for their newly elected Queen.

Amidala smiled and folded her fingers carefully together in her lap. She didn't want to touch the high collar that rose past her ears. *It's straight,* she told herself. *It must be straight. Eirtaé checked it before I came in.* The elaborate royal costumes and formal face paint were as much a part of her new position as the decisions she was called upon to make every day. And her appearance was especially important today, because she was about to speak with the Trade Federation. Their representatives, she knew, already thought that a fourteen-year-old girl was far too young to rule a planet. *That's probably why they picked Naboo for their blockade. Well, I'll show them that I'm capable.*

The large view screen lit up, showing the overbearing Trade Federation viceroy, Nute Gunray. "Again you come before me, Your Highness," he said. "The Federation is pleased."

Amidala stiffened. His words were civil, but his tone was . . . insolent. "You will not be so pleased when you hear what I have to say, Viceroy," she said in as cold a voice as she could manage. "Your blockade has ended."

The Neimoidian's mouth twitched into something very like a smirk. "I am not aware of such a failure."

"Enough of this pretense, Viceroy!" Queen Amidala said, allowing her anger to show. She felt a stir of approval from the councilors around her, and went on, "I know that the Chancellor's ambassadors are with you now —"

"I know nothing about any ambassadors," the viceroy said smoothly. "You must be mistaken."

Surprised, Amidala leaned forward and studied the screen closely. But she could not read the Neimoidian's expression. "Beware, Viceroy," she said at last. "The Federation is going too far this time." *He can't ignore representatives from the Supreme Chancellor! And the Senate will not put up with this blockade for much longer.*

"Your Highness, we would never do anything without the approval of the Senate," Nute said earnestly. "You assume too much."

*Is he acting, or does he mean what he says?* "We

will see," Amidala said, and signaled to end the transmission.

As the screen went black, a buzz of discussion rose from the councilors. Amidala tapped her fingers on the arm of her throne, thinking. After a moment, she turned to the Governor of Theed. "Governor Bibble! Contact Senator Palpatine at once." Palpatine represented Naboo in the Senate of the Galactic Republic. If things had changed on Coruscant, if the ambassadors had not been sent after all, Palpatine would surely know the reason.

But when they reached Senator Palpatine a few moments later, he seemed as bewildered by the viceroy's assertions as everyone else was.

"How could it be true?" he said. "I have assurances from Chancellor —" The communication hologram flickered, then steadied. "His ambassadors did arrive. It must be —" The hologram flickered again, and began to break up.

"Senator Palpatine!" Amidala said urgently. She needed his advice and his experience; he *had* to come through clearly.

"— get — negotiate —" The hologram sputtered and died completely.

Amidala turned to her dark-skinned head of security. "Panaka, what's happening?"

"A malfunction in the transmission generators?" Governor Bibble suggested doubtfully.

"It could be the Federation, jamming us, Your Highness," Captain Panaka said.

"But — but that can mean only one thing!" Sio Bibble said. "An invasion!"

Amidala's heart sank. "The Federation would not dare go that far!" she said, as much to convince herself as to contradict Bibble. She hated the very idea of wars and fighting. They denied everything Naboo stood for.

Captain Panaka nodded. "If they invaded us, the Senate would revoke their trade franchise," he pointed out.

*That's right,* Amidala thought. *And without their trade franchise, they'll lose most of their trading rights in the Outer Rim Territories. Surely they wouldn't take such a risk.* "We must continue to rely on negotiation," she said with renewed firmness.

"Negotiation?" Bibble said in a tone of disbelief. "How can we negotiate? We've lost all communications! And where *are* the Chancellor's ambassadors?"

Amidala had no answers for him.

*It is a good thing most droids have no imagination,* Qui-Gon thought as he crept through the service vent. *And a good thing the Trade Federation depends on droids to do so much for them.* A team of Humans would have searched the service vents long ago. He reached the end of the vent and looked out cautiously as Obi-Wan joined him.

They had come out at one end of a giant hangar, packed with H-shaped landing craft and huge Multi Troop Transports. As they watched, rank after rank of battle droids marched up to the transports and folded themselves into deployment racks. The folded droids made surprisingly small bundles; hundreds of them could fit on a single MTT. As each transport filled, it moved onto one of the landing craft.

"It's an invasion army," Obi-Wan said after a moment.

Qui-Gon nodded. "It's an odd play for the Trade Federation, though." They must have intended all along to invade Naboo; these droids hadn't been brought all this way on a whim. He looked seriously at his apprentice. "We've got to warn the Naboo and contact Chancellor Valorum."

Obi-Wan nodded. "But how?"

"Those are landing craft," Qui-Gon said, gesturing at the ships on the far side of the MTTs. "Let's split up. We'll stow away aboard separate ships and meet down on the planet."

Obi-Wan gave the battle droids a sidelong look. Qui-Gon could guess what he was thinking. If the Jedi were detected, they'd face hundreds of droids at once — enough to overwhelm even their formidable abilities. *But we haven't got much choice. We'll just have to be very, very quiet.*

"You were right about one thing, Master," Obi-Wan said slyly. "The negotiations were short."

*More battle humor.* Qui-Gon snorted. Without replying, he slid out of the vent into the shadows around the edge of the hangar. A moment later, he felt Obi-Wan follow. Together, they stole silently toward the landing craft — and the waiting battle droids.

# CHAPTER ③

The early morning mist was just beginning to thin as Jar Jar Binks waded through the Naboo swamp in search of breakfast. Like most Gungans, he preferred to catch his food fresh. The damp air felt good against the reddish ear-flaps that hung halfway down his back, and the murky water was pleasantly warm around his thick toes. All he needed now was —

A gleam of white caught his eye, half-hidden in the swamp ooze. *Oh, goody morning munchen!* Jar Jar thought happily. One wiry arm reached down and retrieved the clam. The shell snapped closed as Jar Jar's hand touched it. Jar Jar settled down to open his meal.

When the shell opened at last, Jar Jar scooped the clam out of the shell with his long tongue, enjoying its delicate flavor and smoothness. *Dissen the life,* he thought. *Goody munchen and no Captain Tarpals making fuss about little accidents.* He looked up, and froze.

A giant *thing* moved through the swamp, a thing like an enormous head without eyes. It was as big as the nightmarish monsters that rose out of the core rifts from time to time. Swamp creatures fled before it. Among the nuna and peko peko ran a tall, bearded Human, scarcely slowed by the water and rutiger tree roots. Even he could not stay ahead of it, though; the thing gained on him steadily. But Jar Jar could see that the monster was not chasing any of the creatures, not even the Human. It was headed straight for him, Jar Jar Binks.

"Noooo!" Jar Jar cried. Unfreezing, he dropped the clamshell and grabbed the Human running past. "Hep me! Hep me!"

"Let go!" the Human shouted, but Jar Jar clung tightly. The Human dragged him through the swamp, while the monster gained rapidly. Just before it reached them, the Human flung them both down in the mud. Jar Jar felt a hot wind against his back, and then the thing had passed by. As he pulled himself out of the mud, he saw the huge creature vanish into the mist.

"Oyi!" he said. In an ecstasy of relief, he hugged the Human who had saved him. "I luv yous!"

The Human left off wringing swamp water out of

his clothes to glare at Jar Jar. "Are you brainless?" he demanded. "You almost got us killed!"

"I spake," Jar Jar said, taken aback. This Human had no right to be insulting, just because he had saved Jar Jar's life. And now that the creature was gone and Jar Jar was no longer so frightened, he could taste traces of fuel in the swamp air. The thing that had chased them had only been some sort of machine, and not a monster from the core after all.

"The ability to speak does not make you intelligent," the Human told him. "Now, get out of here!"

Jar Jar stared as the Human started off. "No, no," he said, following. "Mesa stay." What was that thing Humans said? Oh, yes — "Mesa yous humbule servaunt."

"That won't be necessary," the Human said absently, scanning the mist.

Jar Jar rolled his eyes. *Humans never understanding anything!* He told the man it was demanded by the gods, as a life debt.

The Human did not answer, but he didn't move off again, either. Encouraged, Jar Jar said, "Mesa called JaJa Binkss."

"I have no time for this now," the tall man muttered.

"Say what?" Jar Jar turned to see what he was looking at. Two strange flying machines broke out of the mist. Each carried a creature like a Gungan skeleton, tall and bone-white. They were chasing another Human. This one was younger and had no beard, but he wore the same sort of brown-and-tan robes as the man who had rescued Jar Jar.

"Oh, nooooo!" Jar Jar cried, his voice climbing higher and higher. "Wesa ganna —"

Something knocked him facedown in the mud, and he heard the bearded Human say, "Stay down!"

Jar Jar raised his head, spitting mud and water. "— die!" he finished, just as the flying machine fired two brilliant bolts of light. To Jar Jar's astonishment, a bar of green light appeared in the bearded Human's hand and bounced the shots back at the skeleton-creatures. The creatures and their machines blew up. Sparks and hot metal fell hissing into the swamp. Quiet returned, except for the panting of the Human the machines had been chasing.

"Sorry, Master," the newcomer said after a moment. "The water fried my weapon." He pulled a short, blackened tube from his belt and handed it to Jar Jar's rescuer.

The bearded man examined the tube, then gave the newcomer a severe look. "You forgot to turn your power off again, didn't you?"

The newcomer nodded sheepishly. Jar Jar cocked his head in sympathy as he picked himself up out of the mud. He understood how easy it was to forget things. He'd done it himself, far too often.

"It won't take long to recharge," the bearded man said, handing the tube back to the newcomer. "But I hope you've finally learned this lesson, my young Padawan."

"Yes, Master," the other man said in a subdued tone.

*No more lecturings*, Jar Jar thought. "Yousa sav-ed my again, hey?" he said, hoping to change the subject.

"What's this?" the newcomer said unenthusiastically.

"A local," the bearded man replied. "Let's go, before more of those droids show up."

The offhand dismissal annoyed Jar Jar briefly . . . and then the rest of the man's words sank in. "Mure? Mure, did you spake?" He did not want to see any more machines.

The two men began to run without replying. Jar Jar followed, thinking rapidly. None of his usual hiding places would be safe from the machines. But the machines had hovered above the swamp. They didn't look as if they'd work well underwater. And under the water was — "Ex-squeezee-me, but da moto grande safe place would be Otoh Gunga," he said as they ran. "Tis where I grew up. Tis safe city."

The men stopped running to look at him. "A city!" the bearded man said. "Can you take us there?"

Jar Jar hesitated. Otoh Gunga would be safe for

the Humans, but for him . . . "Ah, will, on second taut — no, not willy." Seeing their surprise, he looked down. "Iss embarrissing, boot — my afraid my've been banished. My forgotten der bosses would do terrible things to my, if my goen back dare."

In the distance, strange noises echoed through the swamp. "You hear that?" the bearded man said. "That's the sound of a thousand terrible things. Heading this way."

"And when they find us, they will crush us, grind us into little pieces, then blast us into oblivion," the second man added with unnecessary emphasis.

"Yousa point is well seen," Jar Jar said with as much dignity as he could manage. "Dis way. Hurry!"

The odd, froglike native led Qui-Gon and his apprentice to the shore of a lake. After warning them not to expect a warm welcome, he leaped high in the air and dove into the water. The two Jedi pulled breath masks from their belt packs and waded in after him.

Sunlight barely penetrated the murky lake water. Less than a meter below the surface, the light began to dim. Soon it was hard to see. As Jar Jar led the two Jedi deeper and deeper, Qui-Gon began to fear that they would lose him in the increasing darkness.

Suddenly Qui-Gon saw a gleam of light ahead.

In another moment, he could make out a string of amber bubbles, shining warm and bright through the dark water. Their rich yellow glow lit the water for meters around. The bubbles varied in size; the largest looked to be nearly seventy-five meters tall. A lacework of metal the color of old bronze topped each globe, helping the walls keep their shape and providing a place to link bubbles together.

As they drew nearer, Qui-Gon could make out buildings inside the bubbles. Gungans walked casually along the streets, while fish swam past a few meters away outside the bubble wall. They had almost reached the bubble city, and Qui-Gon began to look for a door or an air lock. But Jar Jar swam straight toward the side of the bubble — and passed right through it into the city inside. The bubble wall sealed seamlessly behind him. *Permeable hydrostatic membranes,* Qui-Gon thought. *They keep the seawater out, but let people through, so the city doesn't need an air lock. Impressive.* He followed Jar Jar, beginning to hope they would reach the Naboo palace in time after all.

But the bosses of Otoh Gunga were not willing to help. "Wesa no like the Naboo!" the head Gungan, Boss Nass, declared when the Jedi were brought before him. "Un dey no like uss-ens. Da Naboo tink day so smarty. Day tink day brains so big."

Obi-Wan tried to argue, but the bosses did not

want to listen. "Wesa no care-n about da Naboo," Boss Nass said flatly.

Talk was getting them nowhere. *And if we don't reach the capital soon, the Trade Federation's droids will have taken over.* Qui-Gon gestured, reaching out to touch the Gungan's mind. "Then speed us on our way," he said.

"Wesa ganna speed yousaway," the Gungan Boss said, responding readily to Qui-Gon's suggestion. "Wese give yousa una bongo. Da speedest way tooda Naboo tis goen through da core. Now go."

Qui-Gon thanked him and turned away. As they walked toward the exit, Obi-Wan whispered, "Master, what's a bongo?"

"A transport, I hope," Qui-Gon murmured. *Preferably a fast one . . .* He stopped. Jar Jar Binks stood between two guards, wearing handcuffs and plainly waiting for judgment.

Catching Qui-Gon's eye, Jar Jar said, "Ahh . . . any hep hair would be hot."

Obi-Wan frowned. "We are short of time, Master," he objected.

"We'll need a navigator," Qui-Gon said. "This Gungan may be of help." *Besides, we talked Jar Jar into coming here. If it weren't for us, he wouldn't be in trouble.* Qui-Gon turned back to the Gungan bosses. "What is to become of Jar Jar Binks here?"

"Hisen to be pune-ished," Boss Nass said. "Pounded unto death."

Jar Jar moaned. Obi-Wan looked startled, then worried. Plainly, he had not realized how serious Jar Jar's problem was. Qui-Gon studied the head Gungan. "I have saved Jar Jar Binks' life," he told the Boss. "He owes me what you call a life debt." He gestured, nudging the Gungan's mind once more. "Your gods demand that his life belongs to me now."

"Hisen live tis yos, outlaunder," Boss Nass said. "Begone wit him."

Jar Jar looked from one to the other, and shook his head. "Count mesa outta dis! Better dead here den deader in da core . . . Yee guds, whata mesa sayin?"

As the guards removed Jar Jar's handcuffs, Qui-Gon and Obi-Wan exchanged looks. *Traveling through the core doesn't sound much safer than facing the Trade Federation's battle droids,* Qui-Gon thought. *But at least this way, we have a chance of getting to the Naboo Queen before the droids do.*

*If we survive the trip.*

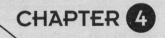

# CHAPTER 4

The hologram of Darth Sidious seemed to make the bridge of the battleship darker, just by being there. Nute glanced around to make sure Lieutenant Dofine was out of sight — there was no sense in annoying the Sith Lord by disobeying his direct order — and said, "The invasion is on schedule, my lord."

"Good. I have the Senate bogged down in procedures. By the time this incident comes up for a vote, they will have to accept your control of the system."

*I wish I were that certain*, Nute thought. "The Queen has great faith that the Senate will side with her," he told Sidious in a neutral tone.

"Queen Amidala is young and naive," Sidious said dismissively. "Controlling her will not be difficult. You have done well, Viceroy."

Nute sighed in relief as the hologram faded away. Dealing with Darth Sidious was almost as nerve-racking as that business with the Jedi had been.

As the last lines of the hologram vanished, Rune Haako turned toward Nute and said, "You didn't tell him about the missing Jedi."

"No need to report *that* to him until we have something to report," Nute said. And he hoped it was good news. He suspected that Darth Sidious wouldn't be nearly so pleased about the success of the invasion, once he learned that the Jedi were missing.

The bongo the Gungans had promised turned out to be a tiny, bat-winged submarine with three bubble canopies and a strange drive that looked like long, trailing tentacles. Obi-Wan eyed it dubiously, but it was better than walking. Or swimming. He slid into the pilot's chair.

"Dis is nutsen," Jar Jar muttered, taking the co-pilot's seat.

Obi-Wan glanced at him in irritation, then looked back at Qui-Gon, who was already sitting in the rear. "Master, why do you keep dragging these pathetic life-forms along with us?"

Qui-Gon only smiled.

The sub arched past tall coral pillars. Reefs stretched away in all directions, like forests made of lace. As the bongo started down into the dark waters below, Obi-Wan flicked a switch and the sub's lights came on. He could see Jar Jar becoming more and more uneasy as they went deeper. *Nervous guides make mistakes; best give him something else to think about.* "Why were you banished, Jar Jar?"

"Tis a longo tale," Jar Jar said. "Buta small part wowdabe, mesa . . . ooooh . . . aaaa . . . clumsy."

"They banished you because you're clumsy?" Obi-Wan asked skeptically. He had seen many different cultures during his years with Qui-Gon, but he had never seen or heard of one with laws against clumsiness.

"Mesa cause-ed mabee one or duey lettal bitty axadentes," Jar Jar said in an offhand tone, waving his arm expansively. "Yud-say boom da gasser, un crash Der Bosses heyblibber. Den —"

Something struck the bongo from behind, causing everyone to jerk forward in their chairs. Obi-Wan looked back and saw a glowing, fishlike creature behind them. It had grabbed the end of the bongo with its long, sticky tongue. The little sub shuddered as the creature began to pull them in.

Jar Jar shrieked. Obi-Wan wrestled with the controls, to no avail. The sea creature drew them closer and closer. Soon its jaws began grinding away at the rear of the sub.

Suddenly, they shot free. Hardly daring to believe their luck, Obi-Wan glanced over his shoulder. The fish that had tried to eat the sub was writhing in the teeth of an even larger sea monster!

"There's always a bigger fish," Qui-Gon commented as Obi-Wan turned back to the controls.

*If it's bigger than that one, I don't want to meet it!* Obi-Wan thought. *No wonder Jar Jar didn't want to come with us.*

As the sub dodged around a coral outcropping and into a tunnel, the lights flickered. Obi-Wan heard a sizzling noise. The giant fish had damaged the bongo. Water was dripping into the cabin, and the power lines were shorting. The sound of the drive lessened, and so did their speed. Obi-Wan pulled a multitool from his belt pack. *This is going to be tricky.* He couldn't shut the power off to work on the lines safely, so if he slipped, the energy would fry him.

Beside him, Jar Jar's voice climbed in panic, but Obi-Wan had no time to soothe the frightened Gungan. Then Qui-Gon's quiet voice said, "Stay calm. We're not in trouble yet."

"What yet?" Jar Jar yelled. "Monstairs out dare! Leak'n in here, all'n sink'n, and nooooo power! You nutsen. WHEN YOUSA TINK WESA IN TROUBLE?!"

Obi-Wan could see Jar Jar's point. He twisted the last wires, wondering whether he would ever attain his Master's unshakable serenity, or feel the Force as clearly and constantly as Qui-Gon. "Power's back," he said.

The lights flickered on as he spoke, revealing yet another enormous fish right in front of them.

"Monstair's back!" Jar Jar countered. "Wesa in trouble now?"

*How many more of these things are there?* Obi-Wan grabbed the controls and swung the ship around. The giant fish-creature darted after them. Obi-Wan increased their speed. The sub shot out of the tunnel — straight toward the huge, eel-like monster that had eaten the first fish!

Jar Jar shrieked again as the monster snapped at the bongo. Obi-Wan dodged, hoping his makeshift repairs would hold. The monster's teeth missed by inches. It snapped again, and its jaws closed around the fish-creature that had chased them through the tunnel. Taking advantage of the distraction, Obi-Wan sent the little sub zipping away.

For what seemed like hours, they wove and ducked and dodged past dozens of huge sea monsters, all of which had one thing in common: They were hungry. At last the water grew lighter, and the monsters fewer. Soon the sub was rising toward the surface.

In a cloud of bubbles, the bongo broke out into open air at last. The engine died, and the sub began drifting with the current. Obi-Wan switched off the bubble canopies, glad to be back in fresh air. He hadn't been entirely sure the sub's power supply would last long enough. They'd even come to the right place — the city of Theed, capital of Naboo, stretched along the shoreline.

Beside him, Jar Jar heaved a sigh of mingled relief and amazement. "Wesa safe now!"

But as they climbed onto shore, a mechanical voice behind them said, "Drop your weapons!"

As one, the Jedi turned. A skeletal Neimoidian battle droid stood threatening them with its lasers. "I said, drop your weapons," it repeated as Jar Jar joined them.

Qui-Gon lit his lightsaber and slashed the droid in half. Obi-Wan stared down at the sizzling wreckage. *They got here before us*, he thought. *This is going to be harder than we hoped.*

The elegant throne room of the Naboo palace was crowded with Trade Federation battle droids. The sight made Amidala want to weep. *I won't cry*, she thought. *I won't give them the satisfaction, even if the guards aren't paying attention to me.* Once she knew that the Trade Federation was really invading, she had switched places with one of her handmaidens. Now her friend and handmaiden Sabé wore the white face paint and the black feathered gown and headdress of the Queen, and Amidala was just . . . Padmé, who wore the same flame-colored robes as the rest of the Queen's handmaiden-bodyguards. "Padmé" did not exist . . . except when Amidala was in disguise. *I hope this works,* she thought. The use of a decoy was established by the rulers before her, but Amidala had never needed it until now.

As they worked their way through the palace, the battle droids brought their captives into the throne room. Amidala could see Governor Bibble and Captain Panaka, along with several of the palace guards. The smug Neimoidian viceroy examined his prisoners with barely concealed satisfaction. He didn't seem to have noticed anything odd about "Queen Amidala." Yet.

"How will you explain this invasion to the Senate?" Sio Bibble demanded when the viceroy looked at him.

"The Naboo and the Federation will sign a treaty," the viceroy said. "I have . . . assurances that the Senate will ratify it." He smiled at the "Queen."

"I will not cooperate," replied Sabé. *She's doing well,* Amidala thought. *She's got my tone of voice down perfectly.*

The viceroy did not seem suspicious. "Now, now, Your Highness," he said patronizingly to Sabé. "You are not going to like what we have in store for your people. In time, their suffering will persuade you to see our point of view."

Amidala ducked her head to hide her expression. *What is he going to do to my people?*

Turning to a nearby battle droid, the viceroy said, "Commander, process them."

"Yes, sir," the battle droid replied. It turned to a group of identical battle droids and said, "Take them to Camp Four."

*Camps. They're herding my people into camps. And we can't stop them; they have more than enough droids to overwhelm our security forces.* One of the battle droids shoved her toward the other handmaidens. Keeping her head lowered, Amidala joined them. *At least the switch worked; they don't know that's not really me. And they can't get a legal treaty without my signature. But . . . but what if the viceroy is right? Can I watch my people starve, and maybe die, and not give in?* Shivering, surrounded by battle droids, Amidala followed the other handmaidens and the "Queen" out of her palace.

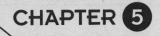 

# CHAPTER 5

From a balcony just outside the Naboo palace, Qui-Gon studied the central plaza of Theed. Flowering vines climbed the golden stone walls. More flowers bloomed pink and red in wrought-iron boxes beneath nearly every window. *The people of Naboo must love living things,* he thought. The graceful arches and domes of the buildings demonstrated their love of elegance as well. The only jarring note, thought Qui-Gon, was the mob of tanks and battle droids assembled in the middle of the plaza.

A group of Humans, guarded by battle droids, came out of the arched entrance to the palace. Several wore the gray-and-red uniforms of the Naboo palace guards. From the pictures he had reviewed at the mission briefing, Qui-Gon identified one of the prisoners as Sio Bibble, Governor of Theed. In the center of the group stood a girl, dressed in an elaborately feathered black costume and wearing royal face paint. She had to be the young Queen of Naboo. Qui-Gon smiled as he signaled to Obi-Wan and Jar Jar.

As the prisoners rounded the corner, the two Jedi jumped down in front of them. "Are you Queen Amidala of the Naboo?" Qui-Gon asked, deliberately ignoring the battle droids.

"Who are you?" the black-clad girl demanded.

"Clear them away!" the commander of the battle droids said.

Qui-Gon watched calmly as four droids stepped forward. He heard the hum of Obi-Wan's lightsaber and ignited his own. An instant later, the droids were nothing but piles of twisted metal. The other battle droids closed in, but they were no match for the Jedi, either. In a few moments there were none left to guard the prisoners.

"Yousa guys bombad!" Jar Jar said admiringly, as the Naboo stared in astonishment.

Qui-Gon put his lightsaber away and bowed to the Queen. "Your Highness, we are the ambassadors for the Supreme Chancellor."

Sio Bibble sniffed and said, "Your negotiations seem to have failed, Ambassador."

"The negotiations never took place," Qui-Gon told him. "Your Highness, we must make contact with the Republic."

"They've knocked out all our communications," a guard wearing a captain's insignia said.

*They'd have been fools not to.* "Do you have transports?" Qui-Gon asked.

"In the main hangar," the captain replied. "This way." He led them down an alley and through the backstreets, to an unguarded service door behind the main hangar. They got inside with no trouble, and they met no droids in the hallways. When they reached the main hangar bay and peered cautiously inside, they found out why. The hangar was full of battle droids.

"There are too many of them," the captain said, shaking his head.

"They won't be a problem," Qui-Gon told him, and looked at the Queen. "Your Highness, under the circumstances I suggest you come to Coruscant with us."

The Queen shook her head. "Thank you, Ambassador, but my place is here."

Qui-Gon started to nod, then stopped as a premonition swept him. "They will kill you if you stay."

"They wouldn't dare!" Sio Bibble said, shocked.

The captain nodded agreement. "They need her to sign a treaty to make this invasion of theirs legal. They can't afford to kill her."

Qui-Gon shook his head. "The situation here is not what it seems, Your Highness. There is no logic to the Federation's move here." Naboo was a small, sparsely populated planet; the Trade Federation wouldn't risk losing their trade franchise by invading it unless there was something else behind their actions. "My feelings tell me they will destroy you," Qui-Gon finished.

Governor Bibble gave Qui-Gon a long, considering look. Then, wearing a thoughtful expression, he turned to the Queen. "Please, Your Highness, reconsider. Our only hope is for the Senate to side with us. Senator Palpatine will need your help."

"No," said the captain. "Getting past their blockade is impossible, Your Highness. The danger is too great."

As the Queen listened to the two men argue, Qui-Gon watched her closely. It was hard to read her expression through her face paint, but he could sense her indecision. Finally she turned to her handmaidens and said, "Either choice presents a great risk — to all of us."

One of the girls stepped forward and gave a tiny nod. "We are brave, Your Highness," she said firmly.

"If you are to leave, Your Highness, it must be now," Qui-Gon put in. He noted with interest that the handmaiden's words seemed to have ended the Queen's indecision.

"Then I will plead our case before the Senate," the Queen said.

Quickly, they sorted out who would come and who would stay behind. Qui-Gon was not surprised when the outspoken handmaiden was among those chosen to accompany the Queen. Several guards and the captain, whose name was Panaka, were also to come with the Queen's party. Two of the handmaidens joined Sio Bibble, who had volunteered to stay and do what he could for the people.

Finally everything was decided. Qui-Gon nodded to Obi-Wan, and they swung the door of the hangar open and strode through. The Queen, her handmaidens and guards, and Jar Jar followed.

The Naboo sense of beauty was evident even in the main hangar bay. The warm golden stone of the walls contrasted nicely with the dark metal of the fueling cables that ran up them. A row of sleek N-1 starfighters sat in their docks along one wall. The center of the hangar was occupied by a silver J-type long-range spacecraft . . . and by a large number of battle droids. More battle droids guarded a group of Naboo men and women in a far corner.

"We need to free those pilots," Captain Panaka said, nodding at the prisoners.

"I'll take care of that," Obi-Wan said. Without

breaking stride, he ducked under a hanging cable and vanished behind a fuel vat.

As Qui-Gon led the rest of the group toward the spaceship ramp, a battle droid stepped in front of him. "Where are *you* going?" it demanded.

Qui-Gon raised his eyebrows. "I'm ambassador for the Supreme Chancellor," he replied in a conversational tone, "and I'm taking these people to Coruscant."

"You're under arrest," the droid said. As it raised its blaster, Qui-Gon cut it down. The Queen and her handmaidens ran past him and up the boarding ramp. More battle droids converged on the ramp. Some of them fired as they came, so that Qui-Gon had to parry the shots in between chopping battle droids in half.

More shots sounded from the corner. Most of the pilots and ground crew ran for the exits; Obi-Wan and one of the pilots made for the royal spaceship. Belatedly, alarms rang through the hangar. As soon as he was certain that everyone was safe, Qui-Gon disposed of his last few opponents and leaped up the ramp.

The ship began to move. "We did it!" one of the guards shouted. "We got away!"

"We're not past the blockade yet," Captain Panaka replied gloomily.

Remembering the cloud of battleships around the

planet, Qui-Gon had to agree. They weren't safe yet, but he had done all he could. As the spaceship accelerated out of the planet's atmosphere, Qui-Gon and Panaka headed for the cockpit.

From here on, it was up to their pilot.

# CHAPTER 6

The royal Naboo spacecraft was the most luxurious ship Obi-Wan had traveled on in a long time, but at the moment, he had no time to appreciate it. Having sent the rescued pilot, Ric Olié, to the cockpit to take off, Obi-Wan made sure that the Queen and her handmaidens were safely in their chamber. Then he stowed Jar Jar in a hold with the astromech droids, where the Gungan couldn't get into much trouble. As he hurried back up toward the cockpit, he felt the ship jolt. *We're already under fire from the blockade battleships!* His stride lengthened.

As he entered the control area, the ship jerked again, and alarms sounded. "We should abort, sir," Ric Olié said to Captain Panaka. "Our deflector shields can't withstand this."

"Stay on course!" Captain Panaka snapped.

The fat ball-within-a-circle battleships grew rapidly larger outside the cockpit windows. There seemed to be twice as many of them as Obi-Wan had seen when he arrived aboard the Republic cruiser. *Of course, it always looks as if there are more of them when they're firing at you.*

The ship rocked as yet another bolt from a Trade Federation battleship exploded against the shields. "Do you have a cloaking device?" Qui-Gon asked.

Panaka shook his head. "This is not a warship. We have no weapons. We're a nonviolent people."

*Which probably has a lot to do with why the Trade Federation attacked them,* Obi-Wan thought. *It's a lot safer to invade someone who isn't likely to fight back.*

Suddenly the ship rocked. *Something must have made it through the shields,* Obi-Wan thought as he straightened.

"Shield generator's been hit," Ric Olié confirmed.

A view screen lit up, showing astromech repair droids popping out of an air lock onto the damaged surface of the ship. "I hope they can fix it," the pilot muttered.

Two Trade Federation fighters swept by, firing at the repair droids. One astromech exploded, then another. Obi-Wan frowned and checked the read-out. Every repair droid on the ship was out there; they had no spares left. "We're losing droids fast," he said.

"We won't make it," Olié said. "The shields are gone."

Another droid exploded. Now the view screen

showed only one left, a small, blue-domed unit. It worked steadily, reconnecting wires despite renewed shots from the fighter droids. Laser blasts whizzed around the little astromech. Several shots missed by barely a hair's breadth. Suddenly, Obi-Wan saw a spray of sparks. For one horrible moment, he thought they had lost the last droid. Then the dazzle cleared from the view screen, and he saw the blue unit heading back toward the air lock. Simultaneously, he heard a whoop of joy from the pilot.

"Power's back!" Olié shouted. "That little droid did it! Deflector shields up, at maximum."

*And just in time,* Obi-Wan thought. They were almost on top of the nearest battleship. For the next few minutes, the firing was intense, but no more shots penetrated the shields. "That's the worst of it," Obi-Wan said as the battleships shrank behind them.

"Maybe not," Olié responded. He pointed at the readouts in front of him. "The hyperdrive is leaking. There's not enough power to get us to Coruscant."

"Then we'll have to land somewhere to refuel and repair the ship," Qui-Gon said calmly. He brought up a star chart on a monitor and stared at it.

Obi-Wan leaned over and tapped the monitor. "Here, Master. Tatooine. The Trade Federation has no presence there."

"How can you be sure?" Captain Panaka asked.

"It's controlled by the Hutts," Qui-Gon replied in an absent tone as he studied the screen.

"The Hutts?" The captain sounded shocked. "You can't take Her Royal Highness there! If the Hutts discovered her —"

"— they'd treat her no differently than the Trade Federation would," Qui-Gon broke in. "Except that the Hutts aren't looking for her, which gives us an advantage."

The captain took a deep, frustrated breath. Obi-Wan suppressed a smile. He'd been on the receiving end of Qui-Gon's relentless logic often enough to sympathize, but this time they really had no choice. Not if they wanted to stay out of the hands of the Trade Federation long enough to get to Coruscant.

"Destroy all high-ranking officials, Viceroy," Darth Sidious commanded. "Slowly and quietly." He paused. "And Queen Amidala — has she signed the treaty?"

Nute Gunray had been dreading that question for hours. "She — she has disappeared, my lord. One Naboo cruiser got past the blockade."

"Find her!" Darth Sidious raged. "Viceroy, I want that treaty signed!"

Nute fought the urge to cringe. *It's only a hologram,*

he told himself. "My lord, it's impossible to locate the ship. It's out of range."

"Not for a Sith Lord," the hooded figure purred. Sidious gestured, and a second hologram appeared behind him — another mysterious cloaked and hooded being. Nute caught a glimpse of bright yellow eyes, and a face tattooed all over in red and black. And were those horns, poking up under his hood? Nute shivered. *I don't think I really want to know.*

"Viceroy, this is my apprentice, Lord Maul," Darth Sidious continued. "He will find your lost ship."

"Yes, my lord," Nute said. The hologram faded, and Nute shook his head. "This is getting out of hand. Now there are two of them!"

"We should not have made this bargain," Rune Haako said glumly. "What will happen when the Jedi learn of these Sith Lords?"

Nute shivered again. He had been wondering about that himself. *At least I don't have to find that ship. That's Lord Maul's job now.*

For some reason, that worried him almost as much as the missing ship.

As soon as the royal Naboo spacecraft was safely in hyperspace, Qui-Gon, Obi-Wan, and Captain Panaka were summoned to the Queen's chamber to bring her up to date. Panaka brought along the little blue-domed repair droid. When they arrived, Qui-Gon let Panaka describe the space battle and the droid's heroism. At the end of his report, the security captain presented the astromech droid to the Queen.

"Without a doubt," Panaka said, "this droid saved the ship. As well as our lives."

The Queen smiled at the little droid. "It is to be commended. What is its number?"

The droid beeped. The captain leaned over. Brushing dirt from the droid's side, he read aloud, "R2-D2, Your Highness."

"Thank you, Artoo-Detoo," the Queen said. "You have proven to be very loyal. Padmé!"

The Queen's favorite handmaiden came forward and bowed.

"Clean this droid up as best you can," the Queen told her. "It deserves our gratitude." She turned back to the captain. "Continue, Captain Panaka."

Panaka glanced toward Qui-Gon and hesitated. Taking advantage of the captain's uncertainty, Qui-Gon stepped forward and said, "Your Highness, we are heading for a remote planet called Tatooine. It's a system far beyond the reach of the Trade Federation. We'll make repairs there, then travel on to Coruscant."

"Your Highness," Captain Panaka put in, "Tatooine is very dangerous. It's controlled by an alliance of gangs called the Hutts. I do not agree with the Jedi on this."

*It's not the first time someone's disagreed with my*

*plans, and I doubt it will be the last,* Qui-Gon thought, amused. But all he said was, "You must trust my judgment, Your Highness."

The Queen exchanged a long look with Padmé. Then she nodded. *That handmaiden has too much influence on the Queen,* Qui-Gon thought. *It could mean trouble.*

*Spaceship no goody place for Gungans,* Jar Jar thought as he poked about in the storage cabinets. Every time he touched something, someone shouted at him to leave it alone. And when they didn't shout, whatever he touched spat springs or sparks or bits of metal, and *then* they shouted. And he had no job here — no clams to dig or subs to guide.

At the back of the cabinet, he found an oilcan. Maybe he could be useful to somebody after all. He picked it up and bounded into the central area of the ship, where the Queen's handmaiden was cleaning up Artoo-Detoo. "Hidoe!" he sang out as he came through the door.

The girl jumped and let out a scream. Artoo whistled reproachfully.

"Sorry," Jar Jar said, embarrassed. "No meanen to scare yousa."

"That's all right," the girl said kindly.

"I scovered oily back dare," Jar Jar said, holding out the oilcan. "Needen it?"

She smiled and took the can. "Thank you. This little guy is quite a mess."

"Mesa JaJa Binkssss," Jar Jar said.

"I'm Padmé," the girl told him. "I attend Her Highness." She looked at him curiously. "You're a Gungan, aren't you?"

Jar Jar nodded. Most Naboo didn't like Gungans any more than Gungans liked them, but this girl seemed nice. *And she not yelling over little mistakings, like everybody else.*

"How did you end up here with us?" Padmé asked.

"My no know," Jar Jar replied. He thought for a moment. "Mesa day starten pitty okeyday, witda brisky morning munchen. Den boom —" He pantomimed the giant, headlike troop transport. "Getten berry skeered, un grabben dat Jedi, and before mesa knowen it — pow! Mesa here." *With spaceships shooting and more dangerness than core monsters. And hyperdrive going bad, and maybe booming everybody before wesa getting to planet.* He shrugged, unable to put it all into words. "Getten berry berry skeered."

# CHAPTER 7

The thing Qui-Gon hadn't expected about Tatooine was the light.

He had visited other desert planets, so he had expected the heat, and the air so dry that it was painful to breathe too rapidly. He had expected the endless yellow sand, the low hiss of the dawn wind, and the seedy atmosphere of the spaceports. But he had not expected the light.

The twin suns were just far enough apart to erase each other's shadows, except beneath the largest cliffs. At dawn and sunset, buildings and people cast long, double shades, but during the main part of the day, everything was drenched in light. It was ironic, Qui-Gon thought, that such a light-soaked planet should be home to so many criminals and outcasts.

Ric Olié had set the Naboo Queen's Royal Starship down on the outskirts of a small spaceport. Mos

Espa, the navigation system called it. After some quick consultation, they agreed that Obi-Wan would stay with the ship to guard the Queen, while Qui-Gon went in search of the parts they needed.

The hyperdrive generator had failed completely as they landed. *It's a good thing it didn't give out between star systems,* Qui-Gon thought, looking down at the mess Obi-Wan had just hauled out of the drive compartment. Perhaps that was what had made him so uneasy, these last few hours . . . but no, he could still feel disquiet in the Force.

He leaned closer, as if to inspect the drive. "Don't let them send any transmissions while we're gone," he said softly to Obi-Wan. "Be wary. I sense a disturbance in the Force."

"I feel it also, Master," Obi-Wan said.

Satisfied, Qui-Gon collected Artoo-Detoo and Jar Jar, and started for the city. They were only a few meters from the boarding ramp when someone shouted. Qui-Gon looked back. Captain Panaka and Padmé, the Queen's handmaiden, walked toward him. He noted with misgiving that Padmé wore rough-spun peasant clothes.

"Her Highness commands you to take her handmaiden with you," Captain Panaka said as he came up to Qui-Gon. "She wishes for her to observe —"

"No more commands from Her Highness today,

Captain," Qui-Gon interrupted, shaking his head. "This spaceport is not going to be pleasant."

"I've been trained in defense," Padmé said. "I can take care of myself."

Qui-Gon eyed her narrowly. This might be the Queen's command, but he sensed that the original idea had come from this girl. The last thing he needed was a spoiled handmaiden to watch out for, but . . . "I don't have time to argue," he said. "But this is *not* a good idea." He gave Padmé a stern look. "Stay close to me."

The girl nodded, and fell into line next to Artoo-Detoo. Artoo whistled happily at her, and Jar Jar smiled.

The twin suns beat down on the little group as they made their way into the city, but Amidala hardly noticed. Everything was so different from Naboo — the dry air, the endless yellow sand, the lumpy buildings of the spaceport — and the heat was only one more difference to wonder at. It had not been easy to convince Captain Panaka to risk letting her come, but she was already glad she had. *As long as everyone thinks I'm plain Padmé, I'm hardly in any more danger than I would be at the ship. And so far, nobody suspects.*

Walking on the loose desert sand was tiring. Even in the city, most of the streets were unpaved, though at least the constant traffic on the busier streets had packed the surface down. Artoo-Detoo didn't seem bothered, but Jar Jar complained bitterly.

Qui-Gon led them to a small open area surrounded by piles of worn-looking equipment and irregular, sand-colored shops. It looked very unpromising to Amidala, but Qui-Gon took a brief look around and nodded. "We'll try one of the smaller dealers," he said, and headed for a little shop with a stack of spaceship parts towering behind it.

As they entered, a pudgy blue-gray alien flew up to them, his wings beating so rapidly that all Amidala could see was a blur. He was only about half as tall as Qui-Gon, but he hovered so that his face was at the same level as the Jedi's.

"Hi chuba da nago?" he said to Qui-Gon.

"I need parts for a J-type 327 Nubian," Qui-Gon replied in Basic.

"Ah, yes," the alien said. When he spoke, his trunk-like nose moved constantly. "Ah, yes, a Nubian. We have lots of that." He shouted something out the rear door of the shop, then turned back to Qui-Gon. "What kinds of parts?"

"My droid here has a readout of what I need," Qui-Gon said, waving at Artoo-Detoo.

A boy ran in through the rear door. He looked about nine years old, with light brown hair. His clothes were rough and ragged. The flying alien spoke to him briefly, then turned to Qui-Gon. "Sooo, let me take thee out back. You'll find what you need."

Qui-Gon and Artoo followed the junk dealer out the back door. Amidala wondered whether she should go with them — Qui-Gon *had* said to stay close. But Jar Jar clearly planned to stay inside, and somebody ought to keep an eye on him. It was all very well for Qui-Gon to say, "Don't touch anything," but Jar Jar was already studying the machines on the shelves with interest. *I'll stay here, for now*, she decided.

The boy seated himself on the counter and began to polish a piece of metal. As he worked, he stared at Amidala. His gaze made her uncomfortable; she caught herself wondering whether she had a smudge on her nose, or a leaf stuck in her hair. *This is ridiculous*, she thought. Forcing a smile, she turned away.

"Are you an angel?"

"What?" Amidala looked back at the boy, startled.

"An angel," the boy said seriously, his blue eyes fixed on her face. "They live on the moons of Iego, I think. They are the most beautiful creatures in the universe. They're good and kind, and so pretty they make even the most hardened space pirate cry."

Amidala was too astonished to answer. Finally, she said, "I've never heard of angels."

The boy studied her, no longer pretending to polish his bits of metal. "You must be one," he said as if it was the most obvious thing in the world. "Maybe you just don't know it."

At home, in the palace, she would have dismissed the remark as mere flattery. But this boy meant every word; somehow, she was sure of it. He felt like a friend she had known all her life — *but I just met him!* "You're a funny little boy," she said. "How do you know so much?"

"I listen to all the traders and pilots who come through here," the boy replied. He gave her a sidelong look. "I'm a pilot, you know. Someday I'm going to fly away from this place."

Amidala couldn't blame him for wanting to leave the heat and the dryness and the mean-looking creatures in the streets outside. But eyeing his ragged clothes, she wondered whether he had any real chance of achieving his dream. "Um, you're a pilot?" she asked.

"All my life," the boy said.

The mental image of a baby in the cockpit of a starfighter made Amidala smile. "Have you been here long?"

"Since I was very little," the boy replied. "Three, I think. My mom and I were sold to Gardulla the Hutt, but she lost us, betting on the Podraces with Watto. Watto's a lot better master than Gardulla, I think."

*Sold? Master? Lost us?* Amidala felt her smile slip. "You're . . . a slave?"

The boy's head came up, and he stuck out his chin. "I am a *person*. My name is Anakin."

"I'm sorry," Amidala said hastily. "I don't fully understand. This is a strange world to me."

A crash made them both jump. Amidala turned to see that Jar Jar had accidentally started up an odd little droid. The droid marched around at random, knocking things over, with Jar Jar clinging to it and shrieking. *Oh, and I was going to watch him!* Amidala thought.

"Hit the nose!" Anakin shouted. Jar Jar did, and the droid stopped and folded itself together. Amidala sighed in relief, then had to laugh at Jar Jar's sheepish expression.

Anakin laughed, too, but sobered quickly. He gave her another of his intent stares and said suddenly, "I'm going to marry you."

Amidala could not help laughing again. *A slave boy, marrying the Queen of Naboo?* But here she was only Padmé, she reminded herself.

At least Anakin did not seem put out by her involuntary laughter. "I mean it," he said seriously.

"You *are* an odd one," Amidala said. "Why do you say that?"

"I guess because it's true."

Something in the boy's manner made Amidala shiver. He seemed so *sure.* "Well, I'm afraid I can't marry you," Amidala told him. "You're just a little boy."

Anakin fixed her with his clear blue eyes. "I won't always be," he said simply.

A cold chill ran down Amidala's back, and she stared at him, unable to think of any response. *He sounds . . . older when he says that. And so positive. What does it mean?*


"Here it is!" the junk dealer cried, hovering in front of a pile of dusty parts. "A T-14 hyperdrive generator! Thee in luck. Saying of which, how's thee going to pay for all this?"

"I have 20,000 Republic dataries," Qui-Gon told him. Finding the parts so quickly meant that they could install the new hyperdrive and get off planet long before —

"Republic credits?" the junk dealer said indignantly. "Republic credits are no good out here. I need something more real."

*There had to be a hitch,* Qui-Gon thought. Luckily, this one was small, and easily dealt with. "I don't have anything else," he told the dealer. Waving his hand in the mind-altering gesture all Jedi learned, he nudged the alien's mind and added, "But credits will do fine."

"No, they won't," the dealer growled, wriggling his nose.

Surprised, Qui-Gon repeated the gesture and nudged harder. "Credits will do fine."

"No, they won't," the dealer said, more loudly than before. "What, you think you're some kind of Jedi, waving your hand around like that? I'm a Toydarian. Mind tricks don't work on me. Only money." He rubbed two clawed fingers together in the universal gesture for cash. "No money, no parts! And no one else has a T-14 hyperdrive, I promise you that!"

He was probably telling the truth. Dealers kept track of one another, and if anyone else had a hyperdrive to sell, this fellow might not have been so stubborn about the credits. Well, perhaps they could trade something from the ship for a new drive. Qui-Gon collected Padmé, Artoo, and Jar Jar, and they left the dealer's shop.

As soon as he found a quiet spot, Qui-Gon called the ship on his comlink. He explained the problem, then said, "You're sure there isn't anything of value left on board?"

Obi-Wan shook his head. "Not enough for you to barter with. Not in the amounts you're talking about."

"All right," Qui-Gon said. "Another solution will present itself. I'll check back." He put his comlink away, and started back out onto the main street.

"Noah gain," Jar Jar said, grabbing his arm. "Wesa be robbed un crunched."

"Not likely," Qui-Gon told him. "We have nothing of value." He sighed. "That's our problem." *And if we can't solve it, we'll be stuck here for a long, long time.*

# CHAPTER 8

Anakin was still thinking about the strangers when he left Watto's junk shop and headed for home. They seemed different from the farmers and smugglers who usually did business with Watto. Especially Padmé. She was . . . even more different than the others. Anakin kicked at the sand. He felt as if he'd known her forever, even longer than all his life. *That's silly*, he thought . . . but it was still the way he felt. And she'd *apologized* to him for calling him a slave. Nobody had ever done that before. *For a while, she made it not matter that I'm a slave. I forgot all about it when I was talking to her.* And she'd been so interested in everything he said. Not even his best friends listened like that. Not even his mom.

Maybe they'd come back to Watto's shop before they left Tatooine. They hadn't bought anything, but Watto hadn't been as grouchy as he usually was when he lost a sale. Maybe it was because he knew nobody else had what they wanted. Maybe they'd *have* to come back before they left the planet.

As he turned onto the market street, Anakin saw one of the strangers ahead of him — the froglike nonhuman one. Sebulba was pushing him around. Anakin swallowed. Sebulba was a Dug, and the biggest bully in Mos Espa. He could use all four arms interchangeably, as long as he left himself one to stand on, so his opponents could never tell where the next blow was coming from. It gave him a big advantage in most fights.

A crowd had gathered to watch. Anakin crushed his fear down until it almost didn't exist, and shoved his way through the crowd. "Careful, Sebulba," he said in Huttese. "This one's very well connected." *If I can get Sebulba to believe that, he'll leave. Nobody messes with the Hutts.*

Sebulba stopped shoving the stranger with any of his hands and glowered at Anakin instead. "Connected? What do you mean, slave?"

"As in Hutt," Anakin said, crushing his anger at being called a slave, just as he had crushed his fear. "Big-time outlander, this one. I'd hate to see you diced before we race again."

"Next time we race, wermo, it will be the end of you," Sebulba snarled. "If you weren't a slave, I'd squash you right now."

"Yeah," Anakin muttered bitterly as Sebulba turned away. "It'd be a pity if you had to pay for me."

As the disappointed crowd started to break up, the rest of the strangers arrived. "Hi!" Anakin said to Padmé. "Your buddy here was about to be turned into orange goo. He picked a fight with a Dug."

"Nosir, nosir," said the alien that Anakin had rescued. "Mesa hate crunchen. Dat's da last ting mesa wanten."

"Nevertheless, the boy is right," the tall, bearded stranger said. "You were heading for trouble." He turned to Anakin. "Thank you, my young friend."

"Mesa doen nutten!" the alien insisted.

"Fear attracts the fearful," Anakin told him. "He was trying to overcome *his* fear by squashing you." The alien stared at him in astonishment. "Be less afraid," Anakin finished.

The tall man gave him a sharp look. Padmé smiled and said, "And that works for you?"

"To a point," Anakin said, returning her smile. His own fear had uncoiled and faded away now that the chance of a fight had passed . . . all but a hard little core. But *that* fear had been with him since the day he was old enough to understand what being a slave meant. He was used to it, and used to hiding it.

Padmé gave him an understanding smile, and for a moment Anakin wondered whether she had fears that had to be crushed sometimes. Then the tall man gestured, and the group continued down the street. They didn't seem to mind that Anakin had joined them.

A little farther along, they stopped at Jira's fruit stand. As he chatted with Jira, Anakin noticed Padmé eyeing the fruit. Struck by sudden inspiration, Anakin said, "I'll take four pallies today, Jira." Turning to Padmé, he added, "You'll like these." He dug in his pocket for the few coins he owned. *Two, three . . . I thought I had four truguts!* Hastily, he pulled the money out to check, and dropped one.

The tall man bent to retrieve it. As he did, his coat shifted, and Anakin glimpsed the handle of a laser sword stuck in his belt. *A lightsaber! He must be a Jedi!* Anakin shifted his gaze quickly. *He must not want people to know, or he'd wear it where everyone could see.*

The Jedi returned Anakin's coin. Anakin had to struggle to keep his voice normal as he said, "Ooops. I thought I had more. Make that three pallies, Jira. I'm not hungry."

The wind was rising, and shopkeepers were taking down their awnings and putting up shutters. "Gracious, my bones are aching," Jira said as she handed Anakin the pallies. "Storm's coming on, Annie. You'd better get home quick."

Anakin looked up at the tall stranger. "Do you have shelter?"

"We'll head back to our ship," he replied.

Anakin hesitated. Even a Jedi wouldn't survive long in a sandstorm. And he might not realize how fast storms came up, or how bad they could be. "Is it far?"

"On the outskirts," Padmé told him.

"You'll never reach the outskirts in time," Anakin said. "Sandstorms are very, very dangerous. Come with me. Hurry!" As soon as he was sure they were following, he headed rapidly for home.

Obi-Wan stood in front of the spaceship, staring across the desert. The wind whipped at his cloak, but he hardly felt it. The Force shook with the same elusive *wrongness* that had been disturbing him since the start of the mission — closer now, but no easier to sense. They needed to get off this planet soon, but there was still no sign of Qui-Gon.

He noticed Captain Panaka and the gathering sandstorm at the same time. "This looks pretty bad," the captain said. "We'd better seal the ship."

Reluctantly, Obi-Wan nodded. Not even Qui-Gon would try to make it to the ship in the middle of a sandstorm. As they turned toward the ramp, the captain's comlink beeped.

It was the pilot, Ric Olié. "We're receiving a message from home."

"We'll be right there," Panaka told him. Obi-Wan was already halfway up the ramp.

The Queen and her handmaiden were watching the transmission when he arrived. The hologram showed the governor, Sio Bibble, and though it faded in and out, the portions that came through clearly were disturbing. ". . . cut off all food supplies . . . death toll . . . catastrophic . . ." And the end was clear, too: "Please tell us what to do! If you can hear us, Your Highness, you must contact me. . . ."

"It's a trick," Obi-Wan said firmly, hoping he was right. "Send no reply." *If we transmit anything, the Trade Federation may trace it back to us. And if they find us, they'll catch us — without a hyperdrive, we're an easy target.*

Captain Panaka and the Queen looked at each other uncertainly. "Send no transmissions of any kind," Obi-Wan repeated, eyeing them until they both nodded.

In the middle of the room, the crackling message began to repeat itself.

Qui-Gon had seen smaller quarters than the slave hovels of Mos Espa, but not many. The shelters were little and stacked tightly; he had to duck to get through the doorway. Ahead of him, he heard the boy Anakin shouting, "Mom! Mom, I'm home!" He smiled slightly. The Force was strong in Anakin, amazingly strong — the boy practically glowed with it. But why had the Force brought Qui-Gon to him? For all his talent, Anakin was already much too old to be trained as a Jedi — Jedi teachers normally worked with very young children, whose emotions had not yet begun to shape their responses. Yet it was clear to Qui-Gon that encountering Anakin was no accident. Best to move slowly, and let things become clearer.

His thoughts were interrupted by the entrance of a dark-haired woman of around forty, presumably Anakin's mother. Her first words confirmed it: "Oh, my! Annie, what's this?"

"These are my friends, Mom," Anakin told her. "This is Padmé, and . . . oh, I don't know any of your names."

Qui-Gon could not help smiling. "I'm Qui-Gon Jinn, and this is Jar Jar Binks."

Beside him, Artoo beeped, and Padmé added, "And our droid, Artoo-Detoo."

"I'm building a droid," Anakin told her eagerly. "You want to see?"

"Anakin!" His mother's tone was sharper than necessary. "Why are these people here?"

"A sandstorm, Mom," Anakin said. "Listen." The howling of the wind had increased, even in the few minutes since they had come inside.

*We made it just in time,* Qui-Gon realized. "Your son was kind enough to offer us shelter," he told Anakin's mother. She still wore a wary, pinched expression, so while Anakin pulled Padmé and Artoo into the next room to see his droid, Qui-Gon dug in his belt pack for food capsules. Handing them to Anakin's mother, he said, "I have enough food for a meal."

"Oh, thank you!" the woman said. Her change in tone and manner told him just how worried she had been about feeding her unexpected visitors, and how little she had to spare. "I'm sorry if I was abrupt," she went on. "I'll never get used to Anakin's surprises."

"He's a very special boy," Qui-Gon said.

The woman gave him a look that was half-startled, half-wary. "Yes," she said softly. "I know." She turned away to begin preparing a meal.

Qui-Gon's comlink beeped. Staring thoughtfully after Anakin's mother, he answered it. It was Obi-Wan, who launched immediately into a description of a disturbing message the ship had just received from Sio Bibble on Naboo. "The Queen is upset," he finished, "but absolutely no reply was sent."

"It sounds like bait to establish a connection trace," Qui-Gon said.

Obi-Wan hesitated. "What if it is true, and the people are dying?"

"Either way, we're running out of time," Qui-Gon said, and cut the link. *If they're trying a connection trace, they must already know that we're on Tatooine. A planet is an awfully large area to search, but even so . . . we haven't much time. And I still have no idea how to get that hyperdrive generator.*

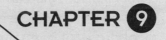

# CHAPTER 9

Anakin's room had the same lumpy, sand-colored walls as every other building Amidala had seen in Mos Espa, and it was almost as full of odd bits and pieces as the junk shop. Anakin dragged her over to a workbench, where a partially completed android lay. Only one eye was finished, and none of its arms or legs had casings yet. "Isn't he great?" Anakin said proudly. Then, a little uncertainly, he added, "He's not finished yet."

"He's wonderful!" Amidala reassured him.

"You really like him?" Anakin said. "He's a protocol droid, to help Mom. Watch!"

He pushed a button, and the droid began to hum. It jerked several times, then stood up.

"How do you do," the droid said in a prim, precise voice. "I am See-Threepio, human-cyborg relations. How may I serve you?"

"He's perfect!" Amidala said, delighted. She had

met plenty of technicians in the palace at home, but she had never known anyone who put a droid together for fun. Anakin really was an amazing boy.

Artoo-Detoo was beeping and whistling at the protocol droid. "I beg your pardon," See-Threepio said to the astromech droid. "What do you mean, I'm naked? What's naked?"

Artoo beeped again, and the protocol droid looked down at himself. "My parts are showing? Oh, my goodness. How embarrassing!"

"Don't worry," Anakin told him. "I'll fix that soon." He turned back to Amidala. "I'm building a Podracer, too! When the storm is over, you can see it."

Amidala could not help smiling at his enthusiasm, though she wondered just what a Podracer was. It sounded a little . . . advanced. Anakin did not seem to notice her puzzlement. Happily, he showed her one incomprehensible gadget after another, until his mother called them to dinner.

Dinner got off to a good start. Anakin's mother — whose name turned out to be Shmi Skywalker — made excellent soup. But then the conversation turned to slavery. As tactfully as possible, Amidala asked why the slaves didn't try to escape.

"All slaves have transmitters placed inside their bodies somewhere," Shmi explained in a matter-of-fact tone.

"I've been working on a scanner to locate them," Anakin put in, "but no luck."

Shmi smiled at him and went on, "Any attempt to escape —"

"— and they blow you up . . . poof!" Anakin finished.

"How wude!" Jar Jar said, horrified.

Without thinking, Amidala said, "I can't believe there is still slavery in the galaxy. The Republic's antislavery laws —"

"The Republic doesn't exist out here," Shmi said sharply. "We must survive on our own."

Deeply embarrassed, Amidala ducked her head. This was all so different from Naboo. A disturbing thought occurred to her — *Is this what is in store for my planet if the Trade Federation's invasion succeeds?*

The silence stretched awkwardly, and then Anakin asked, "Have you ever seen a Podrace?"

Unwilling to chance another mistake, Amidala only shook her head. Beside her, Jar Jar's tongue shot out to snag a plum from a bowl at the far end of the table. Qui-Gon gave him a warning look, then said to Anakin, "They have Podracing on Malastare. Very fast, very dangerous."

"I'm the only human who can do it," Anakin said. His mother gave him a look, and he returned it indignantly. "Mom, what? I'm not bragging. It's true."

"You must have Jedi reflexes if you race Pods," Qui-Gon commented, then demonstrated his own by catching Jar Jar's long tongue as the Gungan attempted to snatch another plum. "Don't do that again," Qui-Gon said, and let the tongue snap back into Jar Jar's mouth.

Anakin stared at Qui-Gon for a moment, then said hesitantly, "I . . . I was wondering — you're a Jedi Knight, aren't you?"

"What makes you think that?" Qui-Gon asked.

"I saw your laser sword," Anakin replied. "Only Jedi carry that kind of weapon."

To Amidala's surprise, Qui-Gon did not seem disturbed by this. He leaned back, and with a slow smile said, "Perhaps I killed a Jedi and stole it from him."

"I don't think so," Anakin said in a positive tone. "No one can kill a Jedi Knight."

An expression of sadness crossed Qui-Gon's face, so quickly that Amidala wasn't even sure she had seen it. "I wish that were so," he murmured, half to himself.

"I had a dream that I was a Jedi," Anakin went on. "I came back here and freed all the slaves." He paused, studying Qui-Gon. "Have you come to free us?"

"No, I'm afraid not," said Qui-Gon.

"I think you have," Anakin said. "Why else would you be here?"

*Oh, no,* Amidala thought. *What can we tell him?* Somehow, she didn't want to lie to Anakin — but he was just a little boy, and they had only just met him. He could already get them in a lot of trouble, if he let the wrong people know that Qui-Gon was a Jedi. They shouldn't make things worse by telling Anakin the truth about why they were on Tatooine.

"I can see there's no fooling you," Qui-Gon said, and leaned forward. "You mustn't let anyone know about us. We're on our way to Coruscant on a very important mission, and it must be kept secret."

"Coruscant? Wow!" said Anakin. "How did you end up out here in the Outer Rim?"

"Our ship was damaged, and we're stranded here until we can repair it," Amidala put in quickly. Qui-Gon was behaving very oddly. There was no telling what else he might let these people know, if she didn't head him off.

"I can help!" Anakin said excitedly. "I can fix any-thing!"

"I believe you," Qui-Gon told him. "But our first job is to acquire the parts we need."

"Wit no-nutten mula to trade," Jar Jar added gloomily.

"These junk dealers *must* have a weakness of some kind," Amidala said.

"Gambling," Shmi said. "Everything here revolves around betting on those awful races."

"Podracing," Qui-Gon said in a thoughtful tone. "Greed can be a powerful ally, if it's used properly."

"I've built a racer!" Anakin said. "It's the fastest ever! There's a big race the day after tomorrow — you could enter my Pod. It's all but finished, and —"

"Anakin, settle down," Shmi said. "Watto won't let you —"

"Watto doesn't know I've built it," Anakin interrupted. He turned to Qui-Gon. "You could make him think it was yours, and you could get him to let me pilot for you."

Shmi's face went stiff. "I don't want you to race, Annie. It's awful."

The strength of Shmi's reaction startled Amidala slightly. Then she remembered what Qui-Gon had said earlier about Podracing. *Very fast, very dangerous.* She shivered, and looked at Anakin.

"But, Mom, I love it," Anakin protested. "And they're in trouble. The prize money would more than pay for the parts they need."

"Wesa ina pitty bad goo," Jar Jar agreed.

"Your mother's right," Qui-Gon said, and Amidala breathed a relieved sigh. The Jedi looked at Shmi. "Is there anyone friendly to the Republic who might be able to help us?"

Slowly, reluctantly, Shmi shook her head.

"We *have* to help them, Mom," Anakin insisted. "You said that the biggest problem in the universe is no one helps each other. You said —"

"Anakin, don't." Shmi's voice was faint.

Anakin broke off. For a moment everyone ate in silence. Finally Amidala could stand it no longer. "I'm sure Qui-Gon doesn't want to put your son in danger," she said to Shmi. "We will find another way."

Shmi sighed. "No, Annie's right. There is no other way." She paused, then went on with difficulty, "I may not like it, but he can help you." She gave Qui-Gon an odd, intent look. "He was meant to help you."

"Is that a yes?" Anakin demanded. "That is a yes!"

Amidala turned to Qui-Gon, expecting him to repeat his refusal, but he only nodded. *I'll have to talk to him later*, she thought. *He can't possibly be serious about this.*

The endless buildings of Coruscant made a twinkling background to Darth Sidious' hologram, but Darth Maul knew better than to be distracted by them. He kept his report brief and accurate, the way Darth Sidious liked them.

"Tatooine is sparsely populated," Darth Maul finished. "If the trace was correct, I will find them quickly, Master." He would have had them already, if they had responded to the message from Naboo. But they had not, and Darth Sidious was never interested in hearing about unsuccessful ploys.

"Move against the Jedi first," Sidious instructed

him. "You will then have no difficulty taking the Queen back to Naboo to sign the treaty."

Darth Maul felt a thrill of anticipation. "At last, we will reveal ourselves to the Jedi. At last, we will have revenge."

"You have been well trained, my young apprentice," Darth Sidious told him. "They will be no match for you." His expression was hidden by his hooded cloak, but his satisfaction was evident in his tone of voice. "It is too late for them to stop us now," he said, half to himself. "Everything is going as planned. The Republic will soon be in my control."

# CHAPTER 10

The following morning, Qui-Gon headed back toward Watto's junk shop. Padmé followed closely, and just as they reached the shop, she stopped him.

"Are you sure about this?" she asked. "Trusting our fate to a boy we hardly know?"

Qui-Gon looked at her without answering.

"The Queen will not approve," Padmé said, as if that settled the matter.

"The Queen does not need to know," Qui-Gon replied simply.

Padmé stared at him, then dropped onto a barrel just outside the shop door. "Well, *I* don't approve," she muttered in a sullen tone.

*And so the little handmaiden discovers that her influence with the Queen has limits,* Qui-Gon thought as he ducked through the doorway into the shop. Still, it was odd that she had been so *very* sure of herself. . . . He heard the sound of an argument, and put Padmé out of his mind.

Watto and Anakin looked up as he entered. "The boy tells me you want to sponsor him in the race," Watto said. "How can you do this? Not on Republic credits, I think!"

"My ship will be the entry fee." Qui-Gon pulled a small hologram projector from his belt pack and triggered it. A small, flickering image of the ship appeared above his hand.

"Not bad," Watto said, examining the projection closely. "Not bad."

"It's in good order, except for the parts we need," Qui-Gon said.

"But what would the boy ride?" Watto said. "He smashed up my Pod in the last race."

Anakin stepped forward quickly. "It wasn't my fault, really! Sebulba flashed me with his port vents. I actually *saved* the Pod. Mostly."

"That you did," Watto said, laughing. "The boy is good, no doubt there."

"I have . . . acquired a Pod in a game of chance," Qui-Gon said blandly. "The fastest ever built."

"I hope you didn't kill anyone I know to get it." Watto laughed again. "So, you supply the Pod and the entry fee; I supply the boy. We split the winnings fifty-fifty, I think."

"Fifty-fifty?" Qui-Gon scoffed. "If it's going to be fifty-fifty, I suggest *you* front the cash for the entry. No, if we win, you keep all the winnings, minus the parts I need. If we lose, you keep my ship." Watto hesitated, and Qui-Gon added persuasively, "Either way, you win."

"Deal!" Watto said at last.

The remaining details were settled quickly. Now that he was committed to the race, Watto was even willing to let Anakin spend the rest of the day getting "Qui-Gon's" Podracer ready. Soon they were all back at the slave quarters. Padmé, Artoo-Detoo, and Jar Jar helped Anakin and his friends work on the Podracer, while Qui-Gon called the ship to let Obi-Wan know of the new plan.

Obi-Wan was hardly more enthusiastic than Padmé had been, but at least he did not try to threaten Qui-Gon with the Queen's displeasure. *Of course, he's known me long enough to realize it would be a pointless thing to do*, Qui-Gon thought.

As he shut off the comlink, Shmi came out onto the porch that ran along the rear of the slave quarters. She watched the excited group around the Podracer for a moment, her expression grave.

Qui-Gon rose and joined her. "You should be proud of your son," he said gently. "He gives without any thought of reward."

"He knows nothing of greed," Shmi said. "He has —" She stopped short and gave Qui-Gon a side-long look, as if she was not sure how much to say.

"He has special powers," Qui-Gon prompted.

"Yes." Shmi's voice was hardly more than a whisper.

"He can see things before they happen," Qui-Gon continued. "That's why he appears to have such quick reflexes. It is a Jedi trait."

"He deserves better than a slave's life."

"The Force is unusually strong with him, that much is clear," Qui-Gon murmured. He could feel that the Force was with this woman, too, though not nearly so strongly as with her son. Where had Anakin gotten such strength? "Who was his father?"

Shmi looked away. "There was no father, that I know of," she said in a low voice. "I carried him, I gave birth . . . I can't explain what happened." When Qui-Gon did not reply, she glanced back and said, "He was special from the very beginning. Can you help him?"

"I'm afraid not," Qui-Gon said, staring down at the Podracer. "Had he been born in the Republic, we would have identified him early, and he would have become a Jedi, no doubt. He has the way. But it's too late for him now. He's too old."

Even as he spoke, he wondered whether that were true.

The Council might make an exception for someone so talented. He was more and more certain that the Force had drawn him to Anakin for some specific purpose.

*    *    *

Anakin had never felt so happy. His Podracer *did* work — well, he'd always known it would, but it was different, actually having the engines ignite for real. He was entered in the Boonta Race, and Padmé would watch him. He would win this time, he knew it. *I have to win. For Padmé.* And he had a real Jedi Knight staying with him, even if it was only for a night or two. With a sigh of contentment, he leaned back to look at the stars.

"Sit still, Annie," said Qui-Gon from beside him. "Let me clean this cut."

The cut was nothing; he'd had hundreds of worse ones. But he couldn't contradict a Jedi. "There are so many stars!" he said instead. "Do they all have a system of planets?"

"Most of them," Qui-Gon replied.

"Has anyone been to them all?"

The Jedi laughed. "Not likely."

"I want to be the first one to see them all," Anakin said. To get away from Tatooine, to go to places where no one knew that he had ever been a slave, to see all the places Padmé must have seen, and more . . . Something pricked his arm. "Ow!"

"There," Qui-Gon said, wiping a patch of blood from Anakin's arm. "Good as new."

"Annie!" his mother shouted from inside. "Bedtime!"

Qui-Gon scraped some of the blood onto a small chip. Anakin stared. "What are you doing?"

"Checking your blood for infections," Qui-Gon said.

Anakin looked at him suspiciously. "I've never seen —"

"Annie!" His mother sounded almost cross. "I'm not going to tell you again!"

She would, though; he had at least one more "last time" call before she got really mad. And he still had a lot of questions . . . but Qui-Gon gestured him inside. "Go on," the Jedi said. "You have a big day tomorrow."

Anakin hesitated. "Good night," Qui-Gon said pointedly.

*Grown-ups!* Anakin rolled his eyes. But there was no getting out of it. He slid down from the porch railing and ran into the house.

Qui-Gon watched until the door closed behind Anakin, then inserted the blood-smeared chip into his comlink and called the ship. Obi-Wan answered at once. "Make an analysis of this blood sample I'm sending you," Qui-Gon told him.

"It'll take a minute," Obi-Wan said.

"I need a midi-chlorian count." The midi-chlorian symbionts channeled the Force to individuals. The more midi-chlorians were present in a person's cells, the more easily that person could sense the Force. Qui-Gon was sure that Anakin's blood would have a high number of midi-chlorians. *The question is how high. . . .*

"All right, I've got it," Obi-Wan said — but he did not continue.

"What are your readings?" Qui-Gon asked after a moment.

"Something must be wrong with the transmission." Obi-Wan sounded uncertain.

Qui-Gon pressed the test button on his comlink. "Here's a signal check."

"Strange," Obi-Wan said after a moment. "The transmission seems to be in good order, but the reading is off the chart — over twenty thousand."

"That's it then," Qui-Gon said with satisfaction. This was why the Force had brought him to Anakin. With a midi-chlorian count like that, the boy *needed* training, no matter how old he was.

"Even Master Yoda doesn't have a midi-chlorian count that high!" Obi-Wan continued.

"No Jedi has," Qui-Gon murmured. *Until now.* But the boy was a slave. How could they get him safely off Tatooine? They couldn't just buy him; they didn't even have enough money to buy hyperdrive parts.

"What does it mean?"

"I'm not sure," Qui-Gon said, and cut off the link. He would have to think about this. Leaning back, he looked out at the stars.

\* \* \*

The long, sinister Sith spacecraft settled to the ground atop a rocky mesa in the Tatooine desert. Darth Maul checked the ship's readouts to make sure no one had detected the landing. There was not much more of Tatooine left to search, and he did not want to lose his prey at the last minute through carelessness. He did not leave the ship until he was satisfied that no detectors were focused in his direction.

Outside, he studied the horizon briefly, then lowered his electrobinoculars. Three more cities to check for the missing Jedi and their spaceship. Only three. *Soon, I will have them.* Two probes per city should be enough to do the job. He punched a code into the control pad on his wrist.

Six black globes floated out of the ship. As they started toward the distant city lights, they split up into pairs, two probe droids per city. Darth Maul watched until they vanished in the darkness. *Soon.*

# CHAPTER 11

The twin suns had just risen when Amidala, dressed once more in Padmé's clothes, came out into the yard to check on the Podracer. She thought she understood Shmi's worries a little better, now that she had gotten a good look at the thing. The Podracer resembled a chariot, pulled by two souped-up Radon-Ulzer Pod engines. Anakin's Pod was tiny, just large enough to hold him and all the controls. His engines, by contrast, were huge — narrow gold machines twice the length of the Podracer, and at least as big around, even with the foils closed.

Artoo-Detoo was still painting the Pod. "I hope you're about finished," Amidala said. Artoo gave a whistle that could only mean *yes*. As she turned away, Amidala saw Anakin's friend Kitster riding toward them on an eopie, leading a second animal behind him. *Time to go*, she thought.

She walked over to Anakin, who was still sleeping soundly beside the Podracer. He looked so young . . . and they were risking everything on him. *If Anakin doesn't win, we'll be stuck on Tatooine. What will become of my people then?* She sighed and touched Anakin's cheek.

Anakin stirred and looked up at her, blinking. "You were in my dream," he said hazily. "You were leading a huge army into battle."

"I hope not. I hate fighting." Amidala felt another little chill run down her spine. What *was* it about this boy that unnerved her so? "Your mother wants you to come in and clean up. We have to leave soon."

Nodding, Anakin stood up. He saw his friend and the eopies, and waved at the Podracer. "Hook them up, Kitster!" he called. Then he looked at Amidala. "I won't be long. Where's Qui-Gon?"

"He and Jar Jar left already," Amidala told him. Anakin nodded and ran inside.

*I do not like this idea of Qui-Gon's,* Amidala thought as she watched him leave. But it was too late for any more objections. They were committed.

Judging from the crowd in the Podracing hangar, the Boonta Race was a very important event. Qui-Gon could see natives of nearly every one of the Outer Rim worlds, from Malastare to Tund. Each of them had brought a custom-designed Podracer and a crew of droids and mechanics to work on them. The prize money for this race must be significant, to attract so many. Watto seemed to take it for granted; he flew alongside Qui-Gon without paying much attention to the racers or their crews.

"I want to see your spaceship the moment the race is over," Watto said as they made their way toward the area assigned to Anakin.

"Patience, my blue friend," Qui-Gon replied. "You'll have your winnings before the suns set, and we'll be far away from here." But with or without Anakin Skywalker? He still had no idea how to free the boy and his mother, though he had spent a considerable part of the night thinking about it. *An opportunity will arise.*

"Not if your ship belongs to me, I think," Watto said. "And I warn you — no funny business."

"You don't think Anakin will win?"

Watto laughed. "That boy is a credit to your race, but Sebulba there is going to win, I think. He always does. I'm betting heavily on Sebulba."

*This is it. This is the chance I've been waiting for.* "I'll take that bet," Qui-Gon said.

Abruptly, Watto stopped laughing. "What? What do you mean?"

"I'll wager my new racing Pod against . . . say . . . the boy and his mother."

"A Pod for slaves?" Watto considered. "Well, perhaps. But just one. The mother, maybe. The boy isn't for sale."

"The boy is small; he can't be worth much," Qui-Gon said persuasively. "For the fastest Pod ever built . . ."

Watto shook his head.

"Both, or no bet," Qui-Gon said. If he could free both of them . . .

Watto shook his head again. "No Pod's worth two slaves, not by a long shot. One slave or nothing."

"The boy, then," said Qui-Gon. Shmi wanted freedom for her son. She would understand. But would Anakin?

Watto pulled a red-and-blue chance cube from his pocket. "We'll let fate decide. Blue it's the boy, red his mother." As he tossed it down, Qui-Gon reached out with the Force and twitched the cube. It landed blue side up. Watto glared, first at the cube, then at Qui-Gon. "You won the small toss, outlander, but you won't win the race," he growled. "So it makes little difference." The thought seemed to cheer him, and he gave a gravelly laugh.

As Watto started toward the grandstand, Anakin's Podracer arrived in a parade of pieces. First came Anakin and Padmé, riding an eopie and dragging one engine behind them; then came Anakin's friend Kitster on a second eopie, dragging the other engine. Last of all, Artoo-Detoo pulled the Pod itself, with Shmi riding in it as if it were a landspeeder.

Watto stopped by Anakin's eopie. "Better stop your friend's betting," Qui-Gon heard him say in Huttese, "or I'll end up owning him, too." Still chuckling, he flew off.

"What did he mean by that?" Anakin asked with a scowl as he dismounted.

"I'll tell you later," Qui-Gon said. No need to put any more pressure on the boy. He had enough riding on his actions already, and he knew how important it was. Qui-Gon could sense the tension within him.

"This is so wizard!" said Kitster, pulling up with the second engine. "I'm sure you'll finish the race this time, Annie."

Padmé looked at Anakin. "You've never won a race? Not even *finished?*" She sounded horrified.

"I will this time!" Anakin said defiantly.

"Of course you will," Qui-Gon told him in a soothing tone. "Let's get this Podracer together." From the corner of his eye, he saw Padmé glaring at him, but the Queen's favorite could wait. Anakin was the one on whom their hopes depended.

As they checked the engines, Qui-Gon felt the dangerous tension within Anakin change slowly to normal excitement. The Jedi breathed a small sigh of relief. Though he did not doubt the power of the

Force, the Force could not act through a mind clouded by fear.

The signal came for the Podracers to take their positions. Anakin joined the row of pilots, while the rest of the group and the eopies hauled his Podracer out into the arena. The grandstand was huge and filled to overflowing. *There must be a hundred thousand beings here,* Qui-Gon thought.

Brightly colored canopies shaded the more expensive seats, and food vendors had set up stands in several places. The racecourse itself swung into the desert and out of sight. Most of the spectators had purchased small, specialized view screens so they could follow every minute of the Podrace. The excitement in the air was catching.

A two-headed Troig announcer began his commentary. Qui-Gon saw several of the sluglike Hutts ooze into a large box near the center of the grandstand. The pilots all bowed to them, while one of the Troig's heads announced, "His honor, our glorious host, Jabba the Hutt has entered the arena."

The Hutt in the center of the box waved to the crowd. As Kitster unhitched the eopies, Jabba began announcing the names and planets of the Podracers. Shmi bent and hugged Anakin tightly. "Be safe," she told him in a tone that was half-command, half-entreaty.

"I will, Mom," Anakin said. "I promise."

Obi-Wan Kenobi, ready to defend.

Queen Amidala of Naboo.

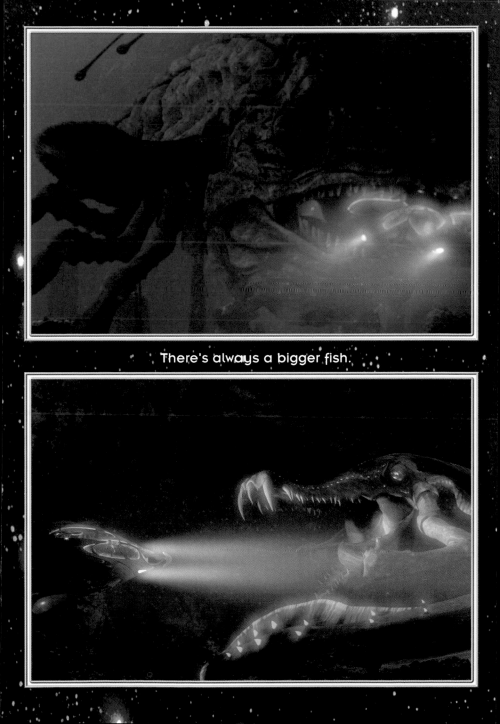

There's always a bigger fish.

Anakin Skywalker, young slave . . . and future Jedi.

Jar Jar, Qui-Gon, and Padmé on the remote, dangerous planet of Tatooine.

Don't try to pay Watto with Republic credits!

Fear attracts the fearful . . . and Jar Jar attracts trouble!

Anakin saves Jar Jar and brings his new friends home.

Artoo-Detoo . . .

. . . meet See-Threepio!

Anakin prepares his Podracer, with a little help from his friends.

It's almost time for the race!

Podracing!

Qui-Gon faces off against the evil Sith, Darth Maul.

There is no emotion; there is peace.

There is no ignorance; there is knowledge.

There is no passion; there is serenity.

There is no death; there is the Force.

Boss Nass, leader of the Gungans.

The battle begins.

A lightsaber duel . . . to the death.

Anakin Skywalker . . . . . . the unexpected hero!

Unsteadily, Shmi walked toward the grandstand. Anakin was already double-checking the cables that held the engines to the Podracer.

". . . Anakin Skywalker tuta Tatooine . . ." boomed Jabba the Hutt's voice, and the crowd roared approval. Anakin waved, then returned to his work. *A good sign*, thought Qui-Gon. *He is not easily distracted.*

It was nearly time for them to go. Qui-Gon gestured for Jar Jar and Padmé to join Shmi in the stands. Jar Jar nodded and turned to Anakin. "Dis berry loony, Annie," he said. "May da guds be kind, mesa palo."

Anakin grinned at him. Padmé came up to him next, and Qui-Gon stiffened slightly. But all she did was kiss Anakin's cheek and say, "You carry all our hopes."

"I won't let you down," Anakin replied with determination.

As Padmé left to join Shmi, the Hutt finished his introductions. The crowd cheered. Qui-Gon helped Anakin into the Podracer and made sure that he was properly strapped in. "Are you all set, Annie?"

Anakin nodded.

Qui-Gon hesitated. "Remember, concentrate on the moment. Feel. Don't think. Trust your instincts." It was as near as he could safely come to telling Anakin to use the Force that flowed so strongly in him. Without training, more specific advice would only confuse the boy. Smiling, Qui-Gon added, "May the Force be with you."

As he walked to the stands to join the others, Qui-Gon heard the roar of dozens of Podracer engines starting.

*It is up to Anakin now.*

# CHAPTER 12

Anakin felt a familiar surge of excitement as his engines began to roar. Excitement, and fear — but Podracing fear was the only kind of fear that felt good. He could forget about Watto, and about being a slave. When he raced, *he* was in control of his fate. If he crashed, if he won, it was because of his own decisions, not his owner's. He had tried to explain to his mother once, but she was so worried about his racing that she didn't really listen.

The starting light flashed green, and Anakin forgot everything but the race. He shoved the control levers, hoping to establish a good position from the very beginning. The Podracer leaped forward . . . and the engines coughed and died.

*No! They can't do this!* Frantically, Anakin worked the controls as Podracer after Podracer swerved around him and vanished into the desert. Finally, he saw the problem — the fuel regulator had been manually adjusted to full open, and the engines had flooded. *How did that happen? Artoo checked it; Kitster checked it; I checked it. . . .* He lost more precious seconds waiting for the extra fuel to evaporate and the engines to start again. At last, they ignited.

Without waiting to see if the engines would keep running, Anakin sent his Podracer screaming after the pack. As he rounded the first turn, he glimpsed a smoking fireball smeared across the base of a rock formation. *Somebody swung too wide and crashed. Got to remember to watch that on the next lap.*

He sped easily through the series of stone arches; without other Podracers getting in his way, they were simple. The trailing Podracers came into view ahead of him. *I'm catching them!* Again, he worked the controls, feeding power first to one engine, then the other. The Podracer swept around the other stragglers, one after another. *If I can get out of this bunch, I can really catch up. . . .*

A Podracer just ahead of him slid sideways, blocking him. Anakin veered to the opposite side, but the other driver seemed to expect it, and cut him off again. And again. Anakin frowned in concentration. *There's a drop coming up — where I wiped out, two races ago.* He pulled back, leaving an extra length between his Podracer and the one that blocked him. Then, just as the other driver went over the drop, Anakin shoved both engine controls full open.

The Podracer surged forward. It flew off the edge of the cliff and over the blocking racer, barely missing the other driver's engines. The Pod came down with a jolt that rattled Anakin's teeth, but a quick check showed all the warning lights still shining green. *It worked! Too bad it happened way out here; I hope Padmé was watching a view screen.*

At the canyon dune turn, he saw another wreck ahead of him. Some instinct made him veer to one side, though he was nowhere close to the burning Podracer. An instant later, a shot bounced off the rear of his Pod.

*Tusken Raiders! Good thing I dodged in time.* He sped up unevenly, trying to make the Podracer a hard target to hit. He must have been successful; no more shots struck his Pod while he was still within range.

The next few racers were strung out along the course. Getting by them was easy, just a matter of speeding up on the turns. Soon he was past all of the stragglers. The grandstand flashed by as he came up on the central pack of racers. *Two laps to go. I can do this!*

It took him most of the second lap to work his way through the pack. Finally, he came within sight of the leading Podracers.

There were only five Podracers ahead of him now. Anakin sped up — and rounded the next corner, right into an enormous cloud of dust. *Somebody else crashed.* He swung wide, hoping to avoid hitting any of the pieces of the smashed racer. One of them hit the Podracer anyway, setting it swinging. Anakin barely compensated in time.

As he came out of the dust cloud, Anakin saw that he'd passed three others. The only racer left ahead of him was Sebulba's — there was no mistaking the odd shape of those engines. *Now I'll show you what a slave can do!* Anakin thought. Leaning forward, he gunned his engines. As the grandstand flashed by for the second time, he came up even with Sebulba. *One more lap. Just one.*

Engine to engine, they raced over the rocky course. A flap opened on the side of Sebulba's near engine, sending a stream of hot exhaust straight at Anakin's engine. *So that's why those other Podracers crashed! Sebulba melted holes in their engines!* Anakin pulled back just in time. Furious at Sebulba's maneuver, he whipped to the inside on the next tight corner and took the lead.

Keeping the lead was harder than taking it had been. Sebulba stayed on Anakin's tail, pushing him on every turn. Anakin clung grimly to his hard-won position. *It's the last lap. I only have to make it through a few more curves. . . .*

Something felt wrong — the left engine. The main inertial compensator was shaking loose. Rapidly,

Anakin adjusted the controls to use the backup system, but he wasn't quite fast enough. While he was changing over, Sebulba passed him.

*I'm not going to lose now!* But every move Anakin made, Sebulba blocked. And there were no more convenient drop-offs coming up; he wouldn't be able to play the same trick he'd used on that other driver, early in the race. *Something else, then . . .*

As they came around the final turn, Anakin pretended to dodge to the inside. It was the same maneuver he had used to pass Sebulba the first time — but when Sebulba dodged to block him, Anakin swung wide, trying to pass on the *outside*.

He did not quite make it all the way around Sebulba's Podracer. Side by side, they headed toward the finish line. Sebulba swerved, deliberately slamming his Pod into Anakin's. He swerved again, and his steering rods became tangled with Anakin's. Anakin fought for control. He could see Sebulba laughing as the finish line drew closer and closer. He tried to unlock the steering rods by pulling away from Sebulba's Podracer, but they were too tightly caught . . . and then Anakin's steering rod broke under the strain.

The Podracer began to spin. Grimly, Anakin hung on to the power controls. No steering, no stability — but he could still change the engines' speed. By instinct and feel, he kept the Podracer on course, heading for the finish line through the cloud of smoke and flame — *smoke and flame? Sebulba crashed?* Anakin crossed the finish line and brought the Podracer to a halt.

As the engines died, he heard cheers and saw Kitster running toward him from the crew pit. Looking back, he saw Sebulba hopping angrily about beside his wrecked Podracer. On the wrong side of the finish line. *Sebulba crashed! I won! I WON!*

Anakin unstrapped himself and stood up. *I never knew winning felt this good,* Anakin thought hazily. *I like this!* He had just time enough to hug Kitster, and then the cheering, chanting crowd swept him up and carried him off on their shoulders.

# CHAPTER 13

Watto was very unhappy about losing his bet. Qui-Gon had to threaten to take the matter to one of the Hutts before the blue alien agreed to provide the parts and release Anakin. While he waited for the junk dealer to deliver the hyperdrive generator, Qui-Gon arranged to borrow the two eopies to haul everything back to the ship. Though the race was over, he still felt uneasy. He wanted the Queen off planet and safely on her way to Coruscant as soon as possible. *The sooner we get the parts back to the ship, the sooner Obi-Wan can start the repairs.*

Obi-Wan was waiting at the ship to help unload, and the work went quickly. Padmé disappeared into the Queen's quarters, presumably to report on her experiences. She took Jar Jar with her.

"I'm going back," Qui-Gon told Obi-Wan as soon as everything was unloaded. "Some unfinished business. I won't be long."

"Why do I sense that we've picked up *another* pathetic life-form?" he asked disapprovingly as Qui-Gon mounted one of the eopies.

*Trust Obi-Wan to pick that up right away.* "It's the boy who's responsible for getting us those parts," Qui-Gon said in what he hoped was a firm, decisive tone.

Obi-Wan rolled his eyes. "Look," Qui-Gon told him, "just get that hyperdrive installed so we can get out of here."

"Yes, Master," Obi-Wan said. "It shouldn't take long."

Still harboring a vague sense of unease, Qui-Gon rode into Mos Espa, leading the second eopie behind him. He visited one of the junk dealers and sold the Podracer for a considerable sum. Then he returned the borrowed eopies and went looking for Anakin.

He found him rolling in the dust with a green-skinned, fishlike Rodian boy. Several other children of various species were watching, wide-eyed. "What's this?" Qui-Gon said.

The fighting stopped abruptly. With wary looks, the two boys climbed to their feet. "He said I cheated!" Anakin said.

"Well, Annie, you know the truth," Qui-Gon said. "You will have to tolerate his opinion. Fighting won't change it."

Anakin gave the Rodian a dark look, but nodded. Then he turned and walked away.

As they neared the slave quarters, Qui-Gon took out the money he had gotten for the Podracer. "These are yours," he said, handing the coins to Anakin. The boy stared, plainly not understanding. "We sold the Pod," Qui-Gon explained.

Anakin's face lit up, and he ran toward home, the fight forgotten. *But how will he feel when he learns that he is free — and his mother is not?* Slowly, Qui-Gon followed.

After all the excitement of the last day, cleaning up had a pleasantly familiar feel to Shmi. The Jedi and his friends would soon be gone, and the race — she tried not to think about the race. It had been wonderful to see Anakin win, but now Watto would want him to race more often. And she couldn't forget the flames rising from the wrecks. *It could have been Annie . . .*

The door banged open, and Anakin ran in. "Mom! Mom, he sold the Pod!" He pulled a fistful of coins from his pocket and shoved them into Shmi's hands. "Look at all the money we have!"

"Oh, my goodness!" Shmi said, staring at the coins. "That's wonderful!" As she hugged Annie, she saw the Jedi standing in the door behind him. She straightened, intending to thank him, and he said quietly, "And Anakin has been freed."

Shmi stared, her mind whirling. She heard at once what Qui-Gon *hadn't* said. Annie was free, but she was not. While Anakin leaped joyfully and hurled excited questions at the Jedi, she struggled to control her feelings. This was what she had asked Qui-Gon, after all — that he help Annie. Now her son had the chance she had always wanted for him. She would have to do her best to see that he took it.

"Now you can make your dreams come true, Annie," she said. "You're free!" Turning to Qui-Gon she asked, "Will you take him with you?" She caught her breath as a dazzling new possibility occurred to her. "Is he to become a Jedi?"

"Our meeting was not a coincidence," Qui-Gon said. "Nothing happens by accident." He looked at Annie. "You are strong with the Force, but you may not be accepted by the Council."

"A Jedi!" Anakin's eyes grew round. "Mighty blasters, you mean I get to go with you in your starship and everything?"

Qui-Gon knelt so that he could look directly into Anakin's eyes. "Anakin, training to be a Jedi will not be easy. And if you succeed, it will be a hard life."

"But it's what I want!" Anakin said. "It's what I've always dreamed about. Can I go, Mom?"

Shmi looked at Qui-Gon, unable to speak. He gave a slight nod of understanding and said to Anakin, "This path has been placed before you, Annie. The choice to take it is yours alone."

Anakin started to answer, then stopped, thinking. He looked at Shmi, then at Qui-Gon. Shmi held her breath. Finally, he said, "I want to go."

"Then pack your things," Qui-Gon said. "We haven't much time."

Elated, Anakin flung his arms around Shmi, then dashed for his room. Suddenly he stopped and looked back, his expression worried. "What about Mom?" he demanded. "Is she free, too? You're coming, aren't you, Mom?"

Qui-Gon looked at Shmi, then turned to Annie once more. "I tried to free your mother, Annie, but Watto wouldn't have it."

"But the money from selling —"

"It's not nearly enough," Qui-Gon said gently.

Annie looked stricken. Shmi sat down next to him and drew him close. "Son, my place is here. My future is here. It's time for you to let go of me. I cannot go with you."

"I want to stay with you," Anakin said in a small voice. "I don't want things to change."

"You can't stop change, any more than you can stop the suns from setting," Shmi said with a sigh. "Listen to your feelings, Annie. You know what's right."

Anakin bowed his head, and Shmi could feel him trembling. Finally, he looked up with tears in his eyes. "I'm going to miss you so much, Mom."

*And I, you, every day and every hour.* "I love you,

Annie," Shmi said, and hugged him tightly for a long moment. "Now hurry."

She watched him run into his room, storing up the sight against the empty days ahead. Then she turned to Qui-Gon. "Thank you."

"I will look after him," the Jedi said. "You have my word." He gazed at her with concern. "Will you be all right?"

Shmi gave a little half-nod and glanced back toward Annie's room. "He was in my life for such a short time," she whispered, almost to herself.

The first probe droid returned hours before Darth Maul expected it — an excellent sign. He checked its readouts with care, and grinned fiercely. *It's the Jedi, all right. On the far side of Mos Espa.* Signaling the droid to use maximum speed, Darth Maul climbed on his speeder and followed it back across the desert.

# CHAPTER 14

It didn't take Anakin long to pack. The only thing he really wanted to bring with him was See-Threepio, but the droid was far too large. He activated Threepio long enough to say farewell, then hurried out to meet Qui-Gon.

Kitster was waiting outside with Shmi, to say good-bye. "Thanks for every moment you've been here," he told Anakin. "You're my best friend."

"I won't forget," Anakin said, feeling hollow. *I have to go. I want to go. I've always wanted to get away from here, but . . . but . . .* He gave Kitster a quick hug and ran toward Qui-Gon, trying to outrun the hurt, to forget about what he was leaving behind. Not just Threepio and Kitster, but all his other friends as well — *they're not here; I won't even get to say good-bye to them.* And his mother . . . He slowed. Stopped. Looked back.

His mother was standing in the doorway, watching him with a sad smile that was more than he could bear. He ran to her, and with tears starting in his eyes, he said, "I can't do it, Mom. I just can't."

She knelt and wrapped her arms around him. He hugged her tightly, and for just a moment everything felt safe and right and ordinary again. Then she sat back and stroked his hair. "Annie, this is one of those times when you have to do something you don't think you *can* do. I know how strong you are, Annie. I know you can do this."

Anakin nodded, not really believing it. "Will I ever see you again?"

"What does your heart tell you?"

"I hope so," Anakin said. Usually, he was certain, the way he had been certain when he told Padmé he would marry her, but this — he wanted this so badly that he couldn't *tell*. "Yes. I guess."

His mother squeezed his arms. "Then we will see each other again."

Anakin swallowed hard. "I . . . I *will* become a Jedi. And I will come back and free you, Mom. I promise."

"No matter where you are, my love will be with you," his mother said. "Now be brave . . . and don't look back." She gave him a little shake, and repeated, "Don't look back."

He gave her one final hug, then turned and marched grimly toward Qui-Gon. *I won't look back,*

*Mom. Watch me. I'm not looking back. I'll make you proud, Mom. I won't look back.*

Silently, Qui-Gon fell into step beside him. The Jedi did not speak until the slave quarters were out of sight behind a building. Then he gestured Anakin to the left. "We have to stop at Watto's shop."

Startled, Anakin looked up. "Why?"

"To get your slave transmitter neutralized."

The process didn't take long, but it left Anakin feeling odd, as if he had suddenly become an entirely new and different person. *I never thought not being a slave would feel so strange*, he thought as he trudged along beside Qui-Gon.

Suddenly, the Jedi spun. His lightsaber hummed out of nowhere. Anakin heard a loud crack, and saw a round, black droid drop in fizzing pieces to the sand. "What is it?" he asked.

"Probe droid," Qui-Gon replied in a grim tone. Bending, he examined the droid more closely. "Very unusual — it's not like anything I've seen before." He stood up and scanned the street, then looked down at Anakin. "Come on." He started running.

Qui-Gon's long legs made it hard for Anakin to keep up, but he did the best he could. He was only a little way behind when the spaceship came into sight. It looked peaceful and normal, but Qui-Gon didn't slow down. "Qui-Gon, sir, wait!" Anakin called.

Qui-Gon turned. His eyes widened and he shouted, "Anakin, drop!"

Without hesitation, Anakin threw himself face-down on the hot sand. He heard a high whine and felt a rush of wind on his back. When he raised his head a moment later, he was just in time to see a man in a black, hooded cloak leap at Qui-Gon from a speeder bike. Swinging a red lightsaber.

*Another Jedi? But a Jedi wouldn't attack Qui-Gon!* Anakin climbed to his feet, watching in confusion as the two men slashed at each other.

"Annie!" Qui-Gon shouted. "Get to the ship! Tell them to take off! Go, go!"

Anakin ran for the ship, hoping he would reach it in time.

"Everything checks out," Ric Olié said as he removed the last test wires. "We can leave as soon as Qui-Gon gets back."

"Good." Obi-Wan wondered why he did not feel more relieved. *Something is very wrong.*

Captain Panaka burst through the cockpit doorway, followed by Padmé and an unfamiliar brown-haired boy. "Qui-Gon is in trouble," the captain said. "He says to take off!"

Olié flung himself at the pilot's chair before Panaka finished speaking. The ship was airborne in moments, without even waiting to close the entry ramp. "I don't see anything," he said as he circled above the desert.

Peering anxiously through the cockpit windows, Obi-Wan spotted a small cloud of dust in the distance. At its center, he felt a great disturbance in the Force — and Qui-Gon. "Over there!" he told Olié. "Fly low!"

The pilot obeyed. The ship skimmed across the surface of the desert, barely a meter above the tops of the dunes. As they came closer, Obi-Wan caught a glimpse of lightsabers flashing amid the dust — *two lightsabers? No wonder Panaka said Qui-Gon was in trouble!* He swallowed hard, hoping that Qui-Gon would see the open entry ramp as the ship passed. He didn't dare use the Force to let his Master know they were coming. In a fight as fierce as that one, even a small distraction could be fatal. *He'll see it. He has to see it.*

As the ship passed over the battle, Obi-Wan felt a surge in the Force. In sudden relief, he let out the breath he hadn't realized he was holding. *He made it!* "Qui-Gon's on board," he told Olié as the ramp closed. "Get us out of here!"

Without waiting to see whether the pilot obeyed, Obi-Wan started for the main hall. The young boy followed him. They found Qui-Gon in a dusty heap just inside the entry, covered with sweat and breathing hard. *I've never seen him in such bad shape after a fight! If we hadn't gotten to him when we did . . .*

"Are you all right?" the boy demanded, voicing part of Obi-Wan's worry.

"I think so," Qui-Gon panted. He sat up, and slowly began to breathe more normally. "That was a surprise I won't soon forget."

"What was it?" Obi-Wan asked.

"I don't know," Qui-Gon replied. "But he was well trained in the Jedi arts."

Obi-Wan blinked. *A renegade Jedi? Impossible!* He caught a look from Qui-Gon that meant "we'll discuss it later," and smothered his questions.

"My guess is that he was after the Queen," Qui-Gon continued.

"Do you think he'll follow us?" the boy asked. He sounded more curious than worried, now that he knew Qui-Gon was not injured.

"We'll be safe enough once we're in hyper-space," Qui-Gon told him. "But I have no doubt that he knows our destination."

"What are we going to do about it?" the boy demanded.

Obi-Wan could not help frowning at the boy. He shouldn't be bothering Qui-Gon like that, especially now. But Qui-Gon did not seem disturbed by the boy's insistent questions. "We will be patient," he said firmly. Then, as if he knew what Obi-Wan had been thinking, he added, "Anakin Skywalker, meet Obi-Wan Kenobi."

"Pleased to meet you," the boy said politely. As he turned to shake hands, he looked straight at Obi-Wan for the first time. His eyes widened. "Wow! You're a Jedi, too?"

The boy's enthusiasm was hard to resist. *But what is Qui-Gon thinking, to get a child mixed up in the middle of a mission? And what will he do with the boy once we get to Coruscant?* Obi-Wan studied Anakin doubtfully. *I don't know about this. I just don't know.*

# CHAPTER 15

*This spaceship is freezing,* Anakin thought. And the coldest part of it was the sleeping quarters. Nobody else seemed to mind; they were all snoring their heads off. But after shivering under the thin blanket for an hour without falling asleep, Anakin gave up. The main area was a little warmer. Surely no one would mind if he curled up in a corner there.

When he got to the main room, he found to his relief that he wasn't the only one who'd thought of sleeping there. Jar Jar was stretched out in a chair, head back, murmuring quietly in his sleep. Artoo-Detoo rested in standby mode next to the wall. Anakin found a corner and sat down.

It was still too cold. No matter how tightly he curled, he didn't feel warm. *This is too different,* he thought miserably. Qui-Gon and Padmé were too busy to talk, and no one else on board cared about him. Well, maybe Jar Jar and Artoo-Detoo. *I shouldn't have come. I should have stayed with Mom. I want to go home!*

A soft sound in the passageway caught his attention. A moment later, Padmé entered the room. She looked tired, and the sadness on her face made Anakin feel even worse than he already did. He shrank back into the corner, hoping she wouldn't see him.

At first, she didn't. She crossed to one of the monitors and switched on a crackly recording of a hologram message. The sound was too low for Anakin to hear clearly, but whatever it was saying made Padmé look sadder than ever. He clenched his teeth to keep them from chattering.

Suddenly, Padmé looked up and saw him. She came over and looked at him with concern. "Are you all right?"

"It's very cold," Anakin admitted, trying to control his shivering.

Padmé *tsk*ed and stripped off her red silk overjacket. "You're from a warm planet, Annie," she said as she tucked it around him. "Too warm for my taste. But space is cold."

Encouraged by her kindness, Anakin said, "You seem sad."

"The Queen is worried," Padmé said softly. "Her people are suffering . . . dying. She *must* convince the Senate to intervene, or . . ." She shook her head. "I'm not sure what will happen."

*How can I help with that?* Anakin thought. *I don't know anything about queens. I guess I'll have to learn.* Suddenly, he felt very lonely. Padmé was the Queen's handmaiden, part of a whole world he knew nothing about. When they reached Coruscant, she would go with the Queen, and he would go . . . wherever people went to be trained as Jedi. But Qui-Gon had said the Council might not accept him. If they didn't —

"I'm — I'm not sure what's going to happen to me," Anakin said in a low voice. "I don't know if I'll ever see you again." He squirmed to get a hand into his pocket, and pulled out the pendant he had been working on. "I made this for you," he said, not daring to look directly at Padmé. "So you'd remember me. I carved it out of a japor snippet." He held it out to her. "It will bring you good fortune."

Padmé took it. After a moment, she said, "It's beautiful, but I don't need this to remember you." Anakin looked up, and she smiled at him. As she hung the pendant around her neck, her expression changed. "Many things will change when we reach the capital, Annie," she said soberly. "But my caring for you will always remain."

"I care for you, too," Anakin told her. "Only — only I miss —" He stopped, blinking back tears.

"You miss your mother." Padmé's voice was soft and gentle and understanding. She leaned forward and gave Anakin a hug. Gratefully, Anakin leaned against her shoulder. It wasn't the same as his mother hugging him, but it was a great comfort. And it was all he had now.

Coruscant resembled a giant pincushion, with its enormous buildings sticking out in all directions like hundreds of needles. Over the centuries, the planet had become a single, giant, multilevel city. The air taxis that ferried citizens from skyscraper to skyscraper made it possible for some people to live their whole lives without ever actually setting foot on the ground. Like the buildings, the taxis were enormous; some of them were as large as cruisers and could hold hundreds of passengers.

Given a choice, Obi-Wan preferred the open spaces of a planet like Tatooine. But Coruscant was the capital of the Galactic Republic, and the home of the Jedi Temple. *And we're lucky we made it back*, he thought as Ric Olié landed the spaceship.

Supreme Chancellor Valorum, current leader of the Republic Senate, was waiting for the Queen on the landing platform. With him was Senator Palpatine, the Naboo representative. The Chancellor was a thin, white-haired man with an air of nervous tension. In contrast, Palpatine stood calm and smiling in his blue Senatorial robes.

Palpatine greeted Queen Amidala smoothly, and

presented the Chancellor. "Welcome, Your Highness," Valorum said. "It is an honor to finally meet you in person. I must tell you how distressed everyone is over the current situation. I've called a special session of the Senate to hear your position."

"I am grateful for your concern, Chancellor," Amidala said, inclining her head gracefully.

Courtesies over, Palpatine motioned Amidala and her guards and handmaidens toward an air taxi at the far end of the platform. As they started off, Obi-Wan heard him say something about procedures. He shook his head ruefully. *She's barely arrived, and he's already talking politics. Well, I suppose that's why she came.*

Then, to Obi-Wan's surprise, the Queen waved at Anakin and Jar Jar to join her. He was about to stop them, when he saw Qui-Gon nod to Anakin. *He arranged this with her before we landed*, Obi-Wan realized.

As the air taxi pulled away, Qui-Gon turned to the Supreme Chancellor. "I must speak with the Jedi Council immediately, Your Honor," he said. "The situation has become . . . more complicated."

*And that's why he didn't want Jar Jar and Anakin with us.* Obi-Wan looked at his Master and frowned. Qui-Gon was worried about something, deeply worried. Something more than the attack in the desert. Obi-Wan could sense it. *What has he not told me?*

\* \* \*

*It is good to be Queen Amidala again*, thought Amidala, but it was also hard. She had not realized how much the responsibility weighed on her mind until she had let go of a tiny fraction of it to become Padmé. Now she knew — but she was still the elected Queen of Naboo, and her people were depending on her. *Why else did I come to Coruscant?* She had taken back her proper role as the ship entered Coruscant's atmosphere; now she sat with Senator Palpatine, planning their presentation to the Galactic Senate.

Senator Palpatine had put more than half his living quarters at his Queen's disposal. The rooms were as lavish as the royal palace on Naboo — and a great relief after the cramped quarters on the Royal Starship. Too much of a relief, perhaps; Amidala found it difficult to concentrate on what Palpatine was telling her.

"The Republic is not what it once was," Palpatine said as he paced the floor before her. "There is no interest in the common good — no civility, only politics. It's disgusting." He paused and said in a heavy tone, "I must be frank, Your Majesty. There is little chance the Senate will act on the invasion."

Amidala frowned, startled. "Chancellor Valorum seems to think there is hope."

"If I may say so, Your Majesty, the Chancellor has little real power," Palpatine said. "The bureaucrats are in charge now."

*If that is true, then this whole trip has been wasted effort.* Amidala pressed her lips together. *I will not let it be wasted.*

"What options do we have?" she asked.

"Our best choice would be to push for the election of a stronger Supreme Chancellor," Palpatine said. "You could call for a vote of no confidence in Chancellor Valorum."

"But he has been our strongest supporter." To force him out of office would feel like betraying him. She couldn't do it . . . but to save her people? Her planet? "Is there any other way?"

"We could submit a plea to the courts."

"There's no time for that," Amidala said. The courts took even longer to decide things than the Senate. Remembering Governor Bibble's message, she went on, "Our people are *dying*, Senator. We must do something quickly to stop the Federation."

Palpatine shook his head. "To be realistic, Your Highness, I'd say we are going to have to accept Federation control. For the time being."

Amidala stared at him. How could he speak of it so calmly? Perhaps he had been on Coruscant too long; perhaps he had forgotten too much about the ordinary people he represented in the Senate. "That is something I cannot do," she told him. *I will find a way to stop this invasion. Even if I have to face down every bureaucrat on Coruscant to do it.*

\* \* \*

The Jedi Council chambers were located at the peak of the Jedi Temple, just below its crowning spire. The glass walls of the circular room looked out over Coruscant in all directions, interrupted only by the great pillars that supported the spire above. Qui-Gon had been there often over the years, to report on his various missions. Now he and Obi-Wan stood once more before the Jedi Council — twelve Jedi from different planets and different species who guided the whole Jedi order. This time, Qui-Gon's report to them was different. He touched only briefly on the events on Naboo and the Podrace, but he described the fight on the Tatooine dunes in great detail. Then he finished, "My only conclusion can be that it was a Sith Lord."

There was an instant silence. Qui-Gon could feel the Council's shocked surprise. Then Mace Windu, a senior Jedi on the Council, leaned forward, his dark face grim. "A Sith Lord?"

"Impossible!" said Ki-Adi-Mundi, raising his bushy eyebrows almost to his skull ridge. "The Sith have been extinct for a millennium."

On the other side of Mace Windu, Master Yoda's long ears twitched. "The very Republic is threatened, if involved the Sith are."

"I do not believe they could have returned without us knowing," Mace said.

"Hard to see, the dark side is," Yoda responded. Around the Council circle, heads nodded. "Discover who this assassin is, we must."

"I sense he will reveal himself again," Ki-Adi-Mundi said slowly.

"This attack was with purpose, that is clear," Mace Windu said. "And I agree that the Queen is his target."

Yoda turned toward Qui-Gon. "With this Naboo Queen you must stay, Qui-Gon. Protect her."

"We will use all our resources here to unravel this mystery and discover the identity of your attacker," Mace added. "May the Force be with you."

The other Jedi Councilors echoed him, plainly expecting Qui-Gon to leave. Qui-Gon stayed where he was. After a moment, Yoda said in a dry tone, "Master Qui-Gon, more to say have you?"

"With your permission, my Master," Qui-Gon said respectfully. Yoda nodded, and Qui-Gon continued, "I have encountered a vergence in the Force."

The Council stirred. Yoda eyed Qui-Gon narrowly. "A vergence, you say?"

"Located around a person?" Mace Windu asked.

Qui-Gon nodded. "A boy. His cells have the highest concentration of midi-chlorians I have seen in a life-form. It is possible that he was conceived by the midi-chlorians."

Mace Windu sat back. "You refer to the prophecy of the one who will bring balance back to the Force." He gave Qui-Gon a long, skeptical look. "You believe it's this . . . boy?"

"I don't presume —" Qui-Gon began.

"But you do!" Yoda broke in. "Revealed, your opinion is."

"I request the boy be tested," Qui-Gon said stiffly. Whatever they thought of his opinions, he had the right to request that much.

The Council members exchanged looks. Then Yoda said, "Trained as a Jedi, you request for him?"

"Finding him was the will of the Force," Qui-Gon replied firmly. "I have no doubt of that. There is too much happening here. . . ."

"Bring him before us, then," Mace said.

"Tested, he will be," Yoda added in an ominous tone.

Qui-Gon nodded. Bowing, he turned and left the Council chamber.

# CHAPTER 16

The Galactic Senate chambers reminded Amidala just a little of the Tatooine Podracing arena. But instead of a semicircle of viewing stands, ranks of floating platforms hugged the curving walls of the Senate chambers. Each carried representatives and their aides from one of the member planets or organizations; most displayed the symbols or banners of their homeworlds. Sternly, Amidala repressed the urge to gawk. She wasn't here to stare at the Senators, but to persuade them to help Naboo.

Beside her, Senator Palpatine urged her yet again to force a change in the Senate leadership. *He knows more of Coruscant than I do,* Amidala thought. *But Chancellor Valorum has done so much for us. . . . Surely it won't be necessary to force him out of his position.*

From the central pillar, the Chancellor announced that Naboo would address the Senate. The Naboo platform dipped smoothly to take up a position next to the Chancellor's pillar. Amidala's stomach lurched. She was eager to speak.

Senator Palpatine stood and described the history of the dispute between Naboo and the Trade Federation. The Senators from the Trade Federation tried to interrupt, but the Chancellor quashed them. Palpatine finished his remarks and said, "I present Queen Amidala of Naboo, to speak on our behalf."

As Amidala rose to address the Senate, she heard a smattering of applause. "Honorable representatives of the Republic," she began, "I come to you under the gravest of circumstances. The Naboo system has been invaded by force. Invaded — against all the laws of the Republic — by the droid armies of the Trade Fed —"

"I object!" the Trade Federation delegate interrupted loudly. "There is no proof."

*Proof? I was there!* Amidala thought. She opened her mouth to reply, but the Trade Federation Senator went on, "We recommend a commission be sent to Naboo to ascertain the truth."

*A commission? My people are dying! Surely, the Chancellor won't take this proposal seriously!* But other delegates were speaking in favor of the delay, and talking about procedures. And Chancellor Valorum was listening. *Was Palpatine right, after all? If Valorum does not support us . . .*

At last the Chancellor turned back to the assembly. "The point is conceded," he said heavily. "Queen Amidala of Naboo, will you defer your motion in order to allow a commission to explore the truth of your accusations?"

*They didn't even let me finish speaking!* "I will *not* defer," Amidala said angrily. "I have come before you to resolve this attack on our sovereignty *now*." She took a deep breath. "I move for a vote of no confidence in Chancellor Valorum's leadership."

"What?" Valorum said, horrified. "No!"

Around the hall, the delegates murmured in surprise, then began to cheer. In a few moments, the motion had been seconded. The Trade Federation tried to send this motion, too, to a committee, but the rest of the Senate would not cooperate. In unison, the delegates began chanting, "Vote now! Vote now!"

Palpatine leaned toward Amidala. "You see, Your Majesty? The time is with us. Valorum will be voted out, and they will elect a new Chancellor, a strong Chancellor, one who will not let our tragedy continue."

Amidala stared at him. He sounded so certain and so . . . complacent. As if it did not matter that she had been forced to bring down one of Naboo's oldest and strongest supporters. Almost as if he were *pleased* about it.

The vote was set to begin the following day. As the

final arrangements were made, Valorum turned toward the Naboo box. "Palpatine, I thought you were my ally — my *friend*," he said. "How could you do this?"

Palpatine bowed his head almost sadly, but Amidala thought she saw the ghost of a smile cross his face. *He's only pleased because we now have a chance to make the Senate stop the invasion,* she reassured herself. *And we didn't have any other choice. I couldn't let them spend months studying the situation while my people die. I had to call for the vote.* But looking at former Chancellor Valorum, she knew his expression of betrayal would haunt her dreams for a long, long time.

The setting sun washed the balcony outside the Jedi Council chambers with soft color, and tinted the forest of buildings below to match. The view of Coruscant was unequalled. But, Obi-Wan noticed, Qui-Gon was not watching the view. His eyes kept straying toward the Council chambers, where Anakin Skywalker was being tested by the Jedi Council. Obi-Wan sighed.

"The boy will not pass the Council's tests, Master, and you know it," he said. "He is far too old."

"Anakin will become a Jedi," Qui-Gon said with renewed calm. "I promise you."

Did his confidence come from one of the rare

glimpses of the future that sometimes came to Jedi Masters? Or did Qui-Gon plan to train Anakin whether the Council approved or not? Obi-Wan frowned. "Don't defy the Council, Master," he said, half-warning, half-pleading. "Not again."

"I will do what I must."

*He* is *planning to defy them*, Obi-Wan thought with a sinking feeling. "Master, you could be sitting on the Council by now — if you would just follow the Code."

Qui-Gon said nothing. Obi-Wan sighed again. *Qui-Gon can be so stubborn. . . .* "They will not go along with you this time," he warned. *And I don't want to have to watch what will happen then.*

Much to Obi-Wan's surprise, Qui-Gon smiled. "You still have much to learn, my young apprentice," he said quietly.

Uneasily, Obi-Wan turned back toward the city.

The Jedi tests were nothing like what Anakin had expected. Not that he'd actually thought much about what they would be like. *Maybe they're just confusing because I'm older,* he thought. The Jedi Master named Mace Windu had a view screen in front of him, which Anakin couldn't see. As images flashed on the screen, Anakin had to see if he could sense what they were. It was an exhausting challenge — Anakin had no idea how he was doing. Finally, the screen clicked off, and he relaxed a little.

"Good, good, young one," said Master Yoda. "How feel you?"

"Cold, sir," Anakin replied without thinking. He had been cold ever since he left Tatooine, it seemed.

"Afraid, are you?" Master Yoda said.

"No, sir," Anakin said, startled. That wasn't the kind of cold he'd been thinking of at all.

Beside Master Yoda, Mace Windu stirred. "Afraid to give up your life?"

*Oh, that's what they meant.* Anakin hesitated. "I don't think so."

"Be mindful of your feelings," Mace Windu said.

"Your thoughts dwell on your mother," the alien Ki-Adi-Mundi added.

"I miss her," Anakin admitted.

"Afraid to lose her, I think," Master Yoda said almost gleefully.

"What's that got to do with anything?" *Aren't Jedi allowed to have mothers?*

"Everything." Master Yoda's scratchy voice was emphatic. "Fear is the path to the dark side. Fear leads to anger; anger leads to hate; hate . . . leads to suffering."

"I am not afraid!" Anakin said angrily. Did they *want* him to fail?

Master Yoda thrust his head forward, studying Anakin. "A Jedi must have the deepest commitment, the most serious mind. I sense much fear in you."

Anakin took a deep breath. As he had done

before, on Tatooine, he crushed his fear down inside him until it almost did not exist. Almost. Hoping that would be good enough, he raised his chin and said quietly, "I am not afraid."

There was a long pause. Finally, Master Yoda half-closed his eyes and said, "Then continue, we will."

But as Mace Windu picked up the view screen, Anakin could not help wondering whether he had just passed another one of the Jedi tests . . . or failed it.

# CHAPTER 17

As the sky darkened, the lights of Coruscant shimmered on. They made the city look beautiful, Amidala thought, but it was still a cold and artificial place. She had been standing at the window of Palpatine's quarters for half an hour, and she hadn't found a single patch of green. *Coruscant is made of glass and metal. No wonder the Senate is more interested in playing political games than in helping my people.*

Jar Jar Binks joined her by the window, but he seemed more interested in studying her face than in watching the city. "Yousa tinken yousa people ganna die?" he asked.

"I don't know," Amidala answered, feeling hollow. *Only Jar Jar would be so blunt. But . . . I have done all I can do through negotiation and diplomacy. And it hasn't been enough. My people will die if the Republic doesn't send help soon.*

"Gungans ganna get pasted too, eh?" Jar Jar said.

"I hope not." But she sounded unconvincing, even to herself.

Jar Jar must have heard the desperation in her voice, because he said reassuringly, "Gungans no die'n without a fight. Wesa warriors! Wesa gotta grande army." He gave Amidala a sidelong look and added, "Dat why you no liken us, metinks."

Before she could reply, the far door flew open. Captain Panaka and Senator Palpatine hurried in and bowed. "Your Highness," Captain Panaka said, "Senator Palpatine has been nominated to succeed Valorum as Supreme Chancellor of the Galactic Senate!"

"A surprise, to be sure," Palpatine said. "But a welcome one. I promise, Your Majesty, if I am elected, I will bring democracy back to the Republic. I will put an end to corruption."

*Why should I care about democracy and corruption in the Republic, when my people are dying?* But she couldn't say that. "Senator, I fear that by the time you have control of the bureaucrats, there will be nothing left of our cities, our people, our way of life."

Palpatine looked grave. "I understand your concern. But the law is in their favor."

Amidala turned away. "There is nothing more I can do here," she said, half to herself. Coruscant was the Senator's arena. *I am Queen Amidala of*

*Naboo; my place is with my people.* It was time to return home.

"Captain Panaka!" she called. "Ready my ship."

"Please, Your Majesty, stay here, where it is safe," Palpatine said.

"No place is safe, if the Senate doesn't condemn this invasion," Amidala replied somberly, and Palpatine did not contradict her.

The members of the Jedi Council watched with grave expressions as Obi-Wan and Qui-Gon joined Anakin in the center of the chamber. Obi-Wan wondered briefly whether they looked so solemn because Anakin had passed, or because he had failed; then Master Yoda raised his chin and said, "Correct you were, Qui-Gon."

"The boy's cells contain a very high concentration of midi-chlorians," Mace Windu said.

Ki-Adi-Mundi nodded. "The Force is strong with him."

"He's to be trained, then," Qui-Gon said with considerable satisfaction.

The Council members exchanged glances. "No," said Master Windu. "He will not be trained. He is too old; there is already too much anger in him."

*I knew it,* Obi-Wan thought. *And if the Council will not train Anakin, there is nothing more Master Qui-Gon can do.*

"He *is* the chosen one," Qui-Gon insisted, resting his hands comfortingly on Anakin's shoulders. "You must see it."

Master Yoda shook his head. "Clouded, this boy's future is. Masked by his youth."

Qui-Gon took a deep breath. "I will train him then. I take Anakin as my Padawan learner."

Stunned, Obi-Wan jerked his head to face Qui-Gon. *Is this what he had in mind all along?*

Master Yoda frowned. "An apprentice, you have, Qui-Gon. Impossible, to take on a second."

"We forbid it," Mace Windu said flatly.

"Obi-Wan is ready —" Qui-Gon turned to look at Obi-Wan.

*He expects me to help him do this!* Obi-Wan realized. He glared back at Qui-Gon. *Well, if he'd rather be Anakin's Master, let him!* "I am ready to face the trials," he said to the Council.

"Ready so early, are you?" Master Yoda said sarcastically. "What know you of ready?"

"He is headstrong," Qui-Gon said. "And he has much to learn about the living Force, but he is capable. There is little more he will learn from me."

*He means it,* Obi-Wan thought. *He really thinks I'm ready; it's not just because of Anakin. But then why didn't he warn me he was going to do this?*

"Our own counsel will we keep on who is ready," Master Yoda replied. "More to learn, he has."

"Now is not the time for this," Mace Windu broke in. "The Senate is voting for a new Supreme Chancellor, and Queen Amidala has decided to return home. That will put pressure on the Trade Federation."

"And could draw out the Queen's attacker," Master Yoda added.

"Go with the Queen to Naboo and discover the identity of this dark warrior," Mace Windu commanded. "That is the clue we need to unravel this mystery of the Sith."

Master Yoda nodded. "Young Skywalker's fate will be decided later."

Despite himself, Obi-Wan let out a breath of relief. *Later* wasn't a decision that might make Qui-Gon defy the Council. Then he tensed again as Qui-Gon said, "I brought Anakin here. He must stay in my charge. He has nowhere else to go."

"He is your ward, Qui-Gon," Mace answered. "We will not dispute that."

"Train him not," Master Yoda said emphatically. "Take him with you, but train him not!"

"Protect the Queen, but do not intercede if it comes to war," Mace Windu continued. "And may the Force be with you."

Still numb from the decision of the Jedi Council, Anakin waited on the landing platform outside the

Naboo royal starship. He had been so sure that he would be a Jedi . . . now what would he do? Tagging along after Qui-Gon would only remind him of everything he couldn't have. *At least I didn't fail the tests*, he thought. *It's only that I'm too old.* But it was small comfort. And on top of everything, Obi-Wan and Qui-Gon were arguing — about him.

"The boy is dangerous," Obi-Wan told Qui-Gon as they came onto the landing platform. "They all sense it. Why can't you?"

"His fate is uncertain, not dangerous," Qui-Gon replied with a touch of irritation. "The Council will decide Anakin's future. That should be enough for you. Now, get on board."

Reluctantly, Obi-Wan headed up the landing ramp. Anakin looked up as Qui-Gon came over to him. "Master Qui-Gon, sir, I don't wish to be a problem."

"You won't be, Annie," Qui-Gon assured him.

*But I am already*, Anakin thought sadly. *That's why you and Obi-Wan were arguing.*

As if he sensed Anakin's mood, Qui-Gon looked seriously down at him. "I'm not allowed to train you, so I want you to watch me and be mindful," he said. "Always remember: Your focus determines your reality. Stay close to me, and you will be safe."

Anakin nodded, thinking hard. Master Qui-Gon was not allowed to train him, but perhaps he was allowed to answer questions. "Master . . . Sir, I've been wondering," Anakin said. "What are midi-chlorians?"

"Midi-chlorians are a microscopic life-form that resides within all living cells and communicates with the Force," Qui-Gon answered readily.

"They live inside of me?"

"In your cells," Qui-Gon said, smiling. "We are symbionts with the midi-chlorians."

The unfamiliar word made Anakin frown. "Symbionts?"

"Life-forms living together for mutual advantage," Qui-Gon explained. "Without the midi-chlorians, life could not exist, and we would have no knowledge of the Force. They continually speak to you, telling you the will of the Force."

"They do?"

"When you learn to quiet your mind, you will hear them," Qui-Gon told him.

Anakin shook his head. "I don't understand."

Qui-Gon smiled. "With time and training, Annie . . . you will."

*But I'm not allowed to have any training,* Anakin thought as he followed Qui-Gon into the spaceship. *At least maybe I'll see Padmé again. And maybe I can learn some more, if I can figure out the right questions to ask Qui-Gon.* It wasn't as good as being trained to be a Jedi, but it was something.

\*   \*   \*

Outside the Naboo palace, night hid the droids that occupied the city of Theed, making everything look almost as usual. Inside the palace, the cool lights of the throne room made the marble floor gleam . . . except where the communications hologram stood. Nute Gunray looked at the hooded image and shivered. *I'm just a little cold*, he told himself.

"The Queen is on her way to you," Darth Sidious said in his soft, precise voice. "I regret she is of no further use to us. When she gets there, destroy her."

"Yes, my lord," Nute said. Beside him, Rune Haako shifted uneasily. *As soon as we're done, he'll probably lecture me again about how dangerous Darth Sidious is.* But it was too late now to break with the Sith Lord. Far too late.

"Is the planet secure?" Sidious went on.

"Yes, my lord," Nute answered, relieved to have good news. "We have taken over the last pockets of primitive life-forms. We are in complete control now."

"Good," Darth Sidious said. "I will see to it that things in the Senate stay as they are. I am sending Darth Maul to join you. He will deal with the Jedi."

"Yes, my lord," Nute repeated, swallowing hard. The temperature in the throne room really was much too cold; he'd have to have one of the repair droids look at the control system.

The hologram faded. When it was completely

gone, Rune turned to stare at Nute. "A Sith Lord, here? With us?" he said in horror.

"The Naboo Queen is coming back," Nute reminded him. "And the Jedi. Do you want to face them yourself?"

"Of course not! But —"

"The Sith Lord will take care of the Jedi," Nute said. "All we have to do is capture the Queen.

"And destroy her."

# CHAPTER 18

After consulting with Captain Panaka and her handmaiden-bodyguards, Amidala decided that she would become Padmé the handmaiden again as soon as the ship came within reach of the Trade Federation. Until then, she would keep her royal clothes and face paint. She spent most of the voyage back to Naboo in her chambers, thinking about her people, her planet, and the invasion.

None of her advisors believed that returning home was a good idea. Even Qui-Gon Jinn seemed puzzled by her decision. Yet it felt right, as deeply right as defying the Trade Federation in the first place — even though she did not know what she would do when they arrived. Merely sharing her people's fate no longer seemed enough. But how could she fight the vast armies of droids that the Trade Federation possessed?

Armies . . . Jar Jar had spoken of armies. He

seemed sure that his people would fight. Perhaps if the Humans of Naboo had cooperated more with the Gungans, the Trade Federation's invasion would not have succeeded so quickly and easily. Perhaps even now, if they all cooperated . . . But that would mean starting a real war. *The Trade Federation invaded us. Talking and diplomacy haven't helped. Sometimes . . . sometimes you just have to fight back.*

Gradually, an idea took shape in her mind. It would be risky, but Tatooine and the Podrace had taught her something about taking risks. As they neared Naboo, she called her advisors together to tell them her plan.

Captain Panaka had clearly been worrying. "I still don't understand why you insisted on making this trip," he complained. "The moment we land, the Federation will arrest you and force you to sign the treaty."

"I agree," Qui-Gon said. He looked at Amidala. "I'm not sure what you hope to accomplish."

Amidala took a deep breath. "I'm going to take back what's ours."

"There are only twelve of us, Your Highness," Captain Panaka said gently. "We have no army."

Qui-Gon smiled slightly, then shook his head. "And I cannot fight a war for you, Your Highness. I can only protect you."

"I know," Amidala said. She looked over his shoulder, to where Jar Jar stood. "Jar Jar Binks!"

The Gungan looked around, as if he expected someone else to answer. "Mesa, Your Highness?"

"Yes," said Amidala firmly. This was the part she had not dared mention to anyone else until now. The Gungans and the Humans had disliked and misunderstood each other for so long — but if she could persuade Jar Jar, then perhaps she could persuade the rest of his people as well. "I need your help," she told him, and waited with bated breath for his reply.

Anakin spent most of the trip to Naboo in the cockpit with Ric Olié and Obi-Wan, asking questions about the controls. *If I can't be a Jedi, maybe I can be a pilot,* he thought. Olié told him he was a natural, and even Obi-Wan seemed to approve. They actually let him take the copilot's seat once, though there wasn't much piloting to do while the ship was in hyperspace.

Everyone grew tense as they neared Naboo, but when they came out of hyperspace at last, no Trade Federation ships hung between them and the planet. "The blockade is gone!" Captain Panaka said in surprise.

"The war's over," Obi-Wan said. "No need for it now."

"I have one battleship on my scope," Ric Olié said.

Obi-Wan glanced over and nodded. "The Droid Control Ship."

"They've probably spotted us," Captain Panaka said, and his expression grew more worried.

"We haven't much time," Obi-Wan agreed, and the next thing Anakin knew, everyone was preparing to leave the ship. As they gathered in the main hold, waiting for the spacecraft to land, Anakin saw Padmé among the Queen's handmaidens.

"Padmé!" he called joyfully, running over. *I haven't seen her since we got to Coruscant!* "Where have you been?"

"Annie!" Padmé said in surprise. "What are you doing here?"

"I'm with Qui-Gon," Anakin said, and looked down. "But . . . they're not going to let me be a Jedi. I'm too old."

"This is going to be dangerous, Annie," Padmé told him.

"Is it?" Anakin said. "I can help! Where are we going?"

"To war, I'm afraid," Padmé said with a sigh. "The Queen has had to make the most difficult decision of her life. She doesn't believe in fighting, Annie." Her voice became pensive, and she added, almost to herself, "We are a peaceful people. . . ."

"I *want* to help," Anakin assured her. He smiled. "I'm glad you're back."

The smile Padmé gave him in return was just a little

preoccupied, but Anakin was so glad to see her that he didn't care.

Ric Olié brought the Naboo Queen's Royal Starship to a smooth landing in the Gungan swamp. As soon as they were down, Obi-Wan went looking for Qui-Gon. During the voyage, there had been some coldness between them because of the argument on Coruscant. Very likely they would soon be in the middle of a war. Obi-Wan wanted to talk to Qui-Gon while he had the chance.

He found Qui-Gon staring out over the Gungan lake, as if he were waiting for the Gungan bosses to emerge from the water at any moment. "Jar Jar is on his way to the Gungan city, Master," Obi-Wan told him a little uncertainly.

Qui-Gon nodded absently. "Good."

"Do you think the Queen's idea will work?"

"The Gungans will not be easily swayed," Qui-Gon answered. "And we cannot use our power to help her." He looked sternly at Obi-Wan.

Obi-Wan hesitated. He had many things he wanted to say: That he had come to know Anakin better during the voyage, that he had begun to see the boy's potential, that he had been wrong to fear that Qui-Gon wanted to dismiss him. "I — I'm sorry for my behavior, Master," he began. "It is not my place to disagree with you about the boy. And . . . I am grateful that you think I am ready for the trials."

For a long moment, Qui-Gon looked at him. Then he smiled. "You have been a good apprentice," he said warmly. "You are much wiser than I am, Obi-Wan. I foresee you will become a great Jedi Knight."

"If I do, it will be because of what you have taught me," Obi-Wan replied.

The surface of the lake bubbled briefly. Jar Jar emerged and came to join them; by the time he arrived, everyone else had gathered, too.

"Dare-sa nobody dare," Jar Jar said. "All gone. Some kinda fight, I tink."

"Do you think they have been taken to camps?" Captain Panaka asked.

"More likely they were wiped out," Obi-Wan said. The Gungans' primitive electropoles would be little help against the blasters of the Trade Federation's droids.

"No," Jar Jar said. "Mesa no tink so. Gungans hiden. When in trouble, go to sacred place. Mackineeks no find them dare."

"Do you know where they are?" Qui-Gon asked.

Jar Jar nodded, and started off into the swamp. Obi-Wan glanced at Qui-Gon, who shrugged and followed. *I hope it's not far,* Obi-Wan thought. *We haven't much time before the Trade Federation droids come looking for us.*

# CHAPTER 19

*So this is Padmé's planet*, Anakin thought as he sloshed through the swamp after Jar Jar. *It's very wet.* The patches of open water were even stranger than the grass-covered hillocks and the tall trees all around. He'd never seen so much water in all his life. Even the air was thick with damp. It felt like breathing soup. Cold soup.

Jar Jar stopped at last under a stand of trees that looked, to Anakin, like every other stand of trees they had passed. "Dissen it," he said, and made an odd chattering noise.

Gungan guards materialized out of the mist, riding creatures like giant, wingless birds. They took the group farther into the swamp, to the ruins of a huge building. Massive heads, carved of stone, stood among the ruins. Everything was half-buried in weeds and muck; some of the heads had sunk up to their eyes in the swamp.

More Gungans appeared all around. Several of them stood on top of one of the heads; from the way they dressed, Anakin could tell they were important. One stepped forward and looked down at the group. "Jar Jar," he said, "yousa paying dis time. Who's da uss-en others?"

The Naboo Queen stepped forward. Padmé, Captain Panaka, and the two Jedi took up positions behind her. Since Anakin had been told to stay near Qui-Gon, he stepped up beside them. *This is great*, he thought. *I can see everything!*

"I am Queen Amidala of the Naboo," the Queen said to the Gungans. "I come before you in peace."

The head Gungan snorted. "Naboo biggen. Yousa bringen da Mackineeks. Day busten uss-en omm. Yousa all bombad. Yousa all die'n, mesa tink."

Captain Panaka looked around nervously as the Gungan guards lowered their electropoles. Qui-Gon and Obi-Wan were still relaxed, though. If they weren't worried, Anakin wasn't, either. *They must have a plan.*

The Queen seemed as uneasy as Captain Panaka, but she continued, "We wish to form an alliance —"

"Your Honor!"

Anakin's head whipped around. *That was Padmé! Why is she interrupting the Queen?*

The head Gungan seemed just as puzzled as

Anakin. "Whosa dis?" he demanded as Padmé came forward to stand next to the Queen.

"I am Queen Amidala," Padmé said with dignity. She pointed at the royally dressed girl beside her and went on, "This is my decoy, my protection . . . my loyal bodyguard."

Anakin stared, openmouthed. *Padmé is the Queen? She can't be the Queen!*

"I am sorry for my deception," Padmé continued, "but under the circumstances, it has become necessary to protect myself." She paused and looked up at the Gungans. "The Trade Federation has destroyed all that we have worked so hard to build. You are in hiding; my people are in camps. I ask you to help us." She hesitated. "No, I beg you to help us."

Padmé dropped to her knees in front of the Gungans. Captain Panaka and his troops gasped, but she ignored them. "We are your humble servants," Padmé told the Gungan Council. "Our fate is in your hands."

Slowly, Captain Panaka and his men also knelt. Qui-Gon and Obi-Wan exchanged glances, then went down on one knee. Anakin joined them, still feeling stunned. *Padmé is the Queen of Naboo?*

After a moment, the head Gungan began to laugh. "Yousa no tinken yousa greater den da Gungans!" he said. "Mesa like dis. Maybe wesa bein friends."

Padmé and her troops rose to their feet, smiling. Automatically, Anakin imitated them, but he was hardly aware of what he was doing. His eyes were fixed on Padmé — *Queen Amidala. She's Queen Amidala, not Padmé. She won't have time to talk to me anymore.* He felt hollow, the way he had when he left his mother on Tatooine. Even Qui-Gon's comforting hand on his shoulder didn't help. *She's a Queen, and I'm not even going to be a Jedi. I should never have left home.*

After a brief talk with the Gungan leaders, Amidala sent Captain Panaka out to discover what had been happening on Naboo. Meanwhile, she consulted the Gungan generals. By the time Panaka returned, they had come up with a plan.

"What is the situation?" Amidala asked Captain Panaka as he joined the group.

"Almost everyone is in camps," Panaka replied. "A few hundred police and guards have formed an underground movement. I brought as many of the leaders as I could. The Federation's army is much larger than we thought. And much stronger." He hesitated. "Your Highness, this is a battle I do not think we can win."

Amidala smiled. "The battle is a diversion. The

Gungans will draw the droid army away from the cities. We can enter the city using the secret passages on the waterfall side. Once we get to the main entrance, Captain Panaka will create a diversion so that we can enter the palace and capture the viceroy. Without him, they will be lost and confused."

She turned to Qui-Gon and Obi-Wan, who had stayed silently with her ever since she had revealed her true identity. "What do you think, Master Jedi?"

"The viceroy will be well guarded," Qui-Gon pointed out.

"The difficulty is getting into the throne room," Captain Panaka said. "Once we're inside, we shouldn't have a problem."

"Many Gungans may be killed," Qui-Gon said, looking at Boss Nass.

The Gungan leader shrugged. "Wesa ready to do are-sa part."

"We will send what pilots we have to knock out the Droid Control Ship that is orbiting the planet," Amidala assured him. "If we can get past their ray shields, we can sever their communications, and the droids will be helpless." *It was my idea to bring Gungans into this; the least I can do is keep them all from dying,* she thought.

"A well-conceived plan," Qui-Gon said, nodding. "However, there's great risk. The weapons on your fighters may not penetrate the shields on the Control Ship."

"And if the viceroy escapes, Your Highness, he will return with another droid army," Obi-Wan added.

Amidala put her chin up. "That is why we must not fail to get the viceroy," she told them. "Everything depends on it."

The Trade Federation viceroy does not look happy, thought Darth Maul. But then, reporting bad news to Darth Sidious was enough to make anyone unhappy. At least his master did not seem disturbed by the news that the Queen had returned to gather an army.

"She is more foolish than I thought," was all that Darth Sidious said when Nute Gunray finished his report.

"We are sending all available troops to meet this army of hers," Gunray said. "It appears to be made up of primitives. We do not expect much resistance."

Darth Maul stirred. "I feel there is more to this, my master," he said, ignoring the dark look Nute Gunray gave him. "The two Jedi may be using the Queen for their own purposes."

"The Jedi cannot become involved," Sidious said dismissively. "They can only protect the Queen. Even Qui-Gon Jinn will not break that covenant." He paused, considering. "This will work to our advantage."

"I have your approval to proceed then, my lord?" Nute Gunray asked nervously.

"Proceed," said Darth Sidious. His mouth curled into a small smile below his dark hood. "Wipe them out. All of them."

# CHAPTER 20

The Gungan army began its march before dawn. Amidala left shortly afterward with the little group of Naboo guards, fighter pilots, and repair droids that Captain Panaka had assembled. Qui-Gon and Obi-Wan came with her, and so did Anakin Skywalker. She had abandoned her Padmé disguise completely and wore the burgundy battle uniform of the Naboo rulers.

She led her troops through the passages behind the waterfall and into the city. The streets were silent and empty. Looking at them, Amidala's lips tightened angrily. *This city belongs to my people, and the Trade Federation has taken it away from them. I was right to come back.*

Near the main hangar, the little group split up. Captain Panaka took most of the guards and slipped around to the far side of the plaza, while Amidala, the Jedi, and the pilots slipped closer to the hangar door. As they took up their positions, Amidala saw Qui-Gon lean toward Anakin.

"Once we get inside, Annie, you find a safe place to hide," the Jedi ordered. "And stay there."

"Sure," Anakin said, a little too casually.

Qui-Gon gave him a stern look. "And *stay* there!"

Amidala hoped the boy would listen. She would never forgive herself if anything happened to Anakin. . . . Something moved in the shadows on the far side of the plaza, behind the Trade Federation tanks. Captain Panaka was in position. Raising a small laser light, she signaled to him. A moment later, his troops opened fire on the tanks.

Battle droids and tanks headed for the far side of the plaza, leaving the door to the main hangar clear. Amidala and her forces ran into the hangar and began firing at the battle droids inside. True to their orders, Obi-Wan and Qui-Gon did not attack the droids directly. They used their lightsabers only to deflect laser bolts that were aimed at Queen Amidala. But, Amidala noticed, every shot they deflected bounced back and hit a battle droid. The two Jedi were destroying more droids than all the rest of her people put together.

"Get to your ships!" Amidala commanded, and the pilots and their repair droids ran for the starfighters. *Anakin! Where's Anakin?* She blasted another battle droid into fragments of bone-white metal. *I hope he found somewhere safe, the way Qui-Gon told him to.*

As soon as the hangar door opened, Anakin ducked sideways underneath one of the fighters. It made a good hiding place for the first few minutes, but then the pilots swung up into their ships, and the ships began to take off. Anakin looked around for a better spot to hide, and Artoo-Detoo whistled at him from the rear of a nearby starfighter. Quickly, Anakin glanced around. All the pilots had ships already; this one wouldn't be going anywhere. He ran over and climbed into the cockpit.

After a moment the firing lessened. Cautiously, Anakin peeked over the edge of the cockpit. Qui-Gon, Obi-Wan, and Padmé — *Queen Amidala. She's Queen Amidala* — were heading for the exit with the rest of the Naboo guards. "Hey!" Anakin called. "Wait for me!"

"No, Annie, you stay there," Qui-Gon said as Anakin started to climb out of the fighter. "Stay right where you are."

"But I —"

"Stay in that cockpit," Qui-Gon commanded, and turned back to join the troops.

The hangar door opened. Standing in the doorway was a dark, hooded figure. The Queen's troops scattered. Obi-Wan and Qui-Gon stepped forward,

155

tossing their cloaks aside. "We'll handle this," Qui-Gon said.

The menacing figure in the doorway also threw his cloak aside. Anakin gasped. The man's face was completely covered by a red-and-black tattoo, and instead of hair, short horns protruded from his head. As the Jedi lit their lightsabers, the newcomer pulled out one of his own. When he lit it, red bars of light appeared at both ends. *A two-sided lightsaber.* Anakin stared. The tattooed man grinned fiercely and attacked the Jedi.

Behind Anakin, Artoo whistled urgently. Anakin looked around. Six wheel droids had rolled into the far side of the hangar. As he watched, they rose into their battle positions and began firing at Pad — Queen Amidala. "Oh, no!" Anakin said. "We have to do something, Artoo!"

Artoo whistled, and the ship's systems came on. "Great idea!" Anakin said. "Let's see . . ." He turned the ship to point toward the droids and studied the controls. They were different from the ones Ric Olié had shown him on the Royal Starship, but only a little different. *Where's the trigger?* He pressed a button, and the ship shook. *Ooops, wrong one. Maybe this one?* He tried again, and this time the lasers fired. The explosion wiped out two of the destroyer droids. "Yeah, all right! Droid blaster!"

Anakin looked back over his shoulder. The Jedi

and the man with the double lightsaber were engaged in a fierce battle in the middle of the hangar. They paid no attention to the Queen and her troops, who ran quickly out a door on the far side. *She's safe!*

With Amidala gone, the wheel droids fired at Anakin. *Shields up! Shields up!* Frantically, Anakin thumbed switches, trying to remember Ric Olié's instructions. *Always on the right — shields are always on the right . . .*

Suddenly, the ship began moving. Rapidly. Artoo beeped.

"I *know* we're moving!" Anakin shouted back. "I'll shut the energy drive down." *If I can figure out which switch it is . . . that one there, that's the last one I pushed.* He pressed the button again, hoping it would shut the engine off. Instead, the fighter picked up speed. It headed out of the hangar as if it had a mind of its own. Artoo beeped worriedly.

"I'm not doing anything!" Anakin cried as the ship left the city behind and arrowed toward space.

The Gungan army made a grand sight. Hundreds of armored warriors carrying electropoles rode wingless, birdlike kaadu. Hundreds more marched along on foot. Behind them, heavy, reptilian fambaas trudged steadily forward, carrying the Gungan shield generators. Ammunition wagons carried energy balls that glowed blue through their plasma skins. Now that they were out of the swamp, the long lines of warriors and equipment were easy to see as they crossed the rolling plains.

Jar Jar was not enjoying any of it. He had fallen off his kaadu several times already, and nearly poked one of the other Gungans with his electropole. And his armor was very uncomfortable. *Mesa not goody warrior, mesa think.* But Boss Nass had decided to make him one of the Gungan generals. Now Jar Jar was stuck in the forefront of the Gungan army with General Ceel and the other Gungan leaders. *Mesa not liking this.*

Someone shouted. Jar Jar looked up and saw a row of enormous tanks drawn up on a low ridge in front of the army. *Oie boie. Now wesa starting.*

"Energize the shields!" called General Ceel.

The fambaas plodded forward, each carrying a large generator. Red rays shot out of the generators toward a large dishlike amplifier carried by another fambaa. The amplifier spread the rays out into a protective umbrella, completely covering the Gungan army.

It was just in time. The Trade Federation tanks opened fire just as the energy shield was completed. Jar Jar and the Gungans around him cheered as the shield absorbed the blasts.

The tanks stopped firing and moved aside. Giant

transports moved forward. Their doors opened, and racks of battle droids unfolded. The Gungan army went silent, watching the thousands of droids assemble and march toward them.

At General Ceel's command, the line of Gungans threw their electropoles like spears, knocking over some droids and shorting out others. Jar Jar didn't see whether his actually hit anything, but he hoped it had. With their poles gone, some of the Gungans used slingshots to throw balls of energy at the droids. Others loaded larger gobs of energy goo into mortars that fired into the center of the mob of battle droids.

Jar Jar charged forward as the battle droids reached the energy shield. The next few minutes were very confused, with droids firing and Gungans firing back. Somehow, Jar Jar found himself tangled in the remains of a half-destroyed battle droid. Its blaster was still firing, so Jar Jar tried to keep it pointed at the other droids while he worked himself free; he was a general, after all, so he'd better not shoot any of his own troops.

When he got untangled at last, he looked up and saw wheel droids rolling out of the transports toward the battle. Hundreds of wheel droids. *Thissen very, very bad*, he thought.

Then the wheel droids attacked.

*   *   *

Obi-Wan had never been in such a lightsaber battle before. *So this is a Sith Lord*, he thought fleetingly as he dodged and leaped. It was taking every skill he knew just to stay alive. The Sith Lord seemed to cloud Obi-Wan's use of the Force, making it hard to sense his opponent's moves and counter them in time.

Slowly, the Sith Lord forced Qui-Gon and Obi-Wan back. Out of the hangar and down a long hall they fought, then on into the Theed power generator plant. The Sith Lord leaped from one service catwalk to another, and the two Jedi followed. Qui-Gon was in the lead now, taking the brunt of the attacks. The narrow bridge gave them little room to maneuver. Obi-Wan tried to close in on their opponent, but the Sith Lord twisted and kicked him off the catwalk.

The bridge just below was out of reach. Obi-Wan fell several levels before he landed on another ramp. He looked up, searching for the quickest way to get back to the fight. His Master and the Sith Lord had moved farther along the catwalk. As he watched, Qui-Gon knocked the Sith off the bridge.

The Sith Lord landed heavily two levels down. Qui-Gon leaped after him, but the Sith picked himself up and backed through a small doorway. Obi-Wan ran forward as Qui-Gon darted after their opponent. As he reached the door, a series of laser walls went up all along the hallway on the other side — deadly force fields designed to keep unauthorized people and droids out of the area. Obi-Wan peered down the corridor. There were four laser walls between him and Qui-Gon, and five between Obi-Wan and the Sith Lord.

Through the sheets of laser fire, Obi-Wan saw Qui-Gon calmly sit and begin to meditate. He tried not to think about just how badly his Master might need that rest. After the fight on Tatooine, Qui-Gon had been nearly exhausted. Impatiently, Obi-Wan paced along the edge of the laser wall. It would go down again in a minute or two, and the fight would begin again. *The Sith Lord can't get much farther; there shouldn't be anything at the end of this hall except a melting pit. I'll be able to catch up as soon as the laser walls go down.*

He refused to consider what might happen if he didn't.

# CHAPTER 21

The palace was full of battle droids. Amidala and her troops blasted several groups of them, but there always seemed to be more. "We don't have time for this!" she cried in frustration as they came around a corner to find more battle droids.

"Let's try outside," Captain Panaka said. Turning, he shot out one of the windows. Amidala, Panaka, and about half the troops climbed through; the others, and the Queen's handmaidens, stayed in the hall to hold off the battle droids.

The Trade Federation didn't seem to be watching the outside of the palace. Amidala and her forces fired cables from their ascension guns and hauled themselves up. It was a little tricky, but much easier than fighting off hordes of battle droids. In a few minutes, they had reached the level of the throne room. Panaka shot out another window, and Amidala and the others climbed through into a hallway. The door to the throne room was at the far end. *We've almost made it. . . .*

Suddenly, two destroyer droids appeared on either side of the throne room door. Amidala turned and saw two more at the opposite end of the hall. They were trapped. *Battle droids we can fight, but these — our weapons will get through their shields eventually, but by then, they'll have shot most of us.* Amidala dropped her laser pistol. "Throw down your weapons," she said to Captain Panaka. "They win this round."

"But we can't —"

"Captain, I said throw down your weapons." Amidala stared at him until he and his troops dropped their pistols. The destroyer droids moved forward to escort them into the throne room.

The wheel droids rolled through the Gungan army's energy shield, reshaped themselves into their battle configuration, and began blasting. One of them hit a shield generator. The generator exploded, killing the fambaa that had been carrying it, along with several Gungans.

*Uh-oh,* Jar Jar thought, looking up. The protective shield wavered and began to fall apart.

"Retreat!" shouted General Ceel.

Jar Jar was only too happy to comply. With the rest of the Gungans, he turned and ran. Glancing back, he saw tanks moving up behind the destroyer droids. The Trade Federation droid general had lost no time in taking advantage of the weakened shield. In another moment, the tanks were in among the Gungans, firing steadily.

One of the explosions lifted Jar Jar off the kaadu he was riding. He shrieked as he flew through the air . . . and landed on top of one of the tanks. The tank swung its gun around, trying to knock Jar Jar off, but he clung to the barrel. *At least thisen not shooting Gungans righty now,* he thought. *Oie boie, what mesa thinking? Mesa getting killed here!*

A Gungan warrior rode his kaadu up beside the tank and signaled. Gratefully, Jar Jar jumped down behind him. *Maybe mesa not dying yet, hey?* Another tank shot exploded close by, and Jar Jar flinched. But there were explosions everywhere now.

*That Queen saying her pilots stopping the droids,* Jar Jar thought. *Mesa hoping they hurry. Or wesa losing bombad.*

The starfighter, with Anakin inside, continued to rise. Artoo beeped worriedly.

"The autopilot is *what?*" Anakin replied. He studied the controls. "There *is* no manual override, Artoo! You'll have to rewire it or something."

Artoo beeped that he was trying. Anakin looked up. Ahead, he could see the sharp golden Naboo starfighters buzzing like wasps around a large, circular battleship. *That must be the Trade Federation's Droid Control Ship.* Clouds of droid starfighters had emerged from the Trade Federation ship and were attacking the Naboo craft. And the autopilot was taking them straight into the battle.

"Artoo!" Anakin screamed. "Get us off autopilot!"

Artoo screeched an answer. Hoping it was positive, Anakin flipped a switch and tried the controls. This time, the ship responded. "Yes! I've got control. You did it, Artoo!" Frantically, he pulled on the controls, dodging shots and enemy fighters. *As long as I'm up here, maybe I can get one of them. That'd be something to tell Pad — Queen Amidala!*

But figuring out the strange controls in the middle of a battle was not easy. As much by luck as skill, Anakin dodged and ducked and avoided the Trade Federation droid ships. *Or maybe the Force is with me — maybe that's . . . whoops!* A shot whizzed by, narrowly missing him. Artoo shrieked.

"I *know* this isn't Podracing, Artoo!" Anakin said, just as another shot connected with his ship, sending it into a spin. Anakin struggled to regain control as the ship headed straight for the Trade Federation space station.

Desperately, he hauled on the steering. The ship responded sluggishly. *I'm going to smash into the Droid Control Ship! Wait — there's an opening.*

Anakin aimed for it, trying to kill his momentum. It wouldn't do any good to dodge into the opening if he smashed into a wall on the inside.

The opening was some sort of ship hangar. Anakin had to dodge droids and transports. At last he found the right switch, and the reverse thrusters fired. The crippled starfighter skidded to a stop just short of the rear wall. Anakin heaved a sigh of relief and bent to examine the control panel. "Everything's overheated, Artoo. All the lights are red."

Artoo's answering beep sounded frantic. Cautiously, Anakin peered over the edge of the cockpit. *Battle droids! Lots of battle droids. This is not good.* He ducked back down, wondering how long it would take Artoo to fix the ship.

The deadly laser walls cycled off, and Obi-Wan sprinted down the hall. Ahead, he could see Qui-Gon, already battling the Sith Lord. The two fighters circled the melting pit, aiming terrible blows at each other. *I will make it in time. . . .*

Something flickered at the edge of his vision; the laser walls behind him were closing. Obi-Wan flung himself forward — but not quite far enough. The last laser wall flickered into being just in front of him, so close that he nearly ran straight into the deadly rays. *No!* he thought, but it was too late. He was trapped again, just short of the battle, unable to help Qui-Gon.

Obi-Wan stared through the laser wall. For just an instant, Qui-Gon's opponent seemed to be wearing a black helmet, and Obi-Wan felt a cold chill. *This is wrong, this is all wrong. I'm supposed to be the one fighting the Dark Lord.* Obi-Wan shook his head, trying to clear it. The Sith Lord wasn't wearing a helmet; it was only the light of the laser walls on the black of his tattoo. And Qui-Gon was fighting more fiercely than Obi-Wan had ever seen him fight before. Yet the feeling persisted: *That should be me out there, not Qui-Gon.* Obi-Wan shook his head again. *Won't these laser walls ever come down again?*

Qui-Gon blocked one awful stroke and parried another, then struck back. The Sith Lord blocked — and then slammed the wide handle of his lightsaber into Qui-Gon's chin. Qui-Gon staggered backward, half-dazed from the force of the unexpected blow. The Sith Lord grinned in triumph. Reversing his lightsaber, he struck Qui-Gon through.

Qui-Gon crumpled to the floor.

"NO!" Obi-Wan screamed. The sound echoed strangely, almost as if some other voice had joined his in crying out the same desperate denial. But the laser wall was down at last, and Obi-Wan had no more time for thinking. He leaped forward to face the Sith Lord.

Alone.

# CHAPTER 22

The Neimoidian viceroy was waiting inside the throne room with more battle droids. Amidala looked at him with dislike, and he smiled.

"Your little insurrection is at an end, Your Highness," he said smugly. "Time for you to sign the treaty —"

The door opened again. Sabé appeared, dressed in a uniform identical to Amidala's and wearing royal makeup. Behind her, Amidala could see the ruins of several destroyer droids, and she felt a surge of new hope.

The Neimoidian looked uncertainly from Amidala to her double. Sabé called, "I will not be signing any treaty, Viceroy! You've lost!" Turning, she vanished down the hall.

"After her!" the viceroy shouted. "This one's a decoy!"

As most of the droids rushed out of the room, Amidala crossed slowly to her throne. The viceroy turned back to her. "Your Queen will not get away with this!" he said.

Amidala sank down on the throne as if overcome . . . and pressed the security button. The hidden panel in her desk slid open — and the laser pistols were still inside! She tossed two to Captain Panaka and another officer, then snatched a third for herself and blasted the last of the battle droids.

One of her officers ran toward the open door — *no, toward the door control panel. Good idea.* Amidala hit the switch on her desk that closed the door, and the officer jammed the controls. For the moment, they were safe. "Viceroy, this is the end of your occupation," she said fiercely.

"Don't be absurd," the viceroy said, though he was plainly frightened. "There are too few of you. It won't be long before hundreds of destroyer droids break in here to rescue us."

*Not if my pilots blow up your Control Ship*, Amidala thought. But they hadn't succeeded yet, or the destroyer droids wouldn't be active. *What's keeping them?*

The lights on Anakin's control panel were still red. "The system's still overheated, Artoo," he said softly, hoping the astromech droid would hear . . . and the battle droids surrounding his starfighter wouldn't.

"Where's your pilot?" a mechanical voice outside the ship demanded.

*They haven't seen me!* Anakin thought as Artoo whistled a reply.

"*You're* the pilot?" the battle droid said skeptically. "Let me see your identification!"

The lights on the control panel blinked green. "Yes!" Anakin cried, and started the engine.

"You!" the battle droid called. "Come out of there or we'll blast you!"

"Not if I can help it!" Anakin retorted, flipping the switch to raise his shields.

More battle droids were arriving through the open door at the end of the hangar. *This should stop them!* Anakin fired, first his lasers, then the ship's torpedoes. The lasers hit, but the torpedoes flew over the heads of the droids and through the wide-open doors behind them.

"Darn it, I missed," Anakin muttered. A moment later, he heard an explosion as the torpedoes went off somewhere inside the Droid Control Ship. Through the doors, he caught a glimpse of a large, unidentifiable object beginning to come apart. *At least I did some damage!* "Come on, Artoo. Let's get out of here!"

Swinging the ship around, Anakin gunned the engines. The starfighter roared through the hangar and back out into space, just ahead of a sheet of flame. "Now, this is Podracing!" Anakin shouted. "Whoopee!"

Behind him, the Droid Control Ship began to shake. Fire burst from its ports and windows as it slowly exploded from the inside out. Anakin grinned. *I wish Padmé had seen that!*

Trade Federation battle droids had rounded up the Gungan army. The officers were the first to be captured. "Disa bad," Jar Jar said to General Ceel as they watched. "Berry bombad."

"Mesa hopen dissa working for da Queen," the general replied.

Abruptly, all of the droids paused. Some began to shake. Others ran in circles. A few of the flying machines crashed. Then, suddenly, they all stopped moving completely.

The Gungans stared in frozen surprise. When the droids stayed motionless, the Gungans came slowly forward. Jar Jar pushed one of the battle droids. Like a wobbly statue, it fell over.

"Weirding," Jar Jar said. *The Queen be keeping her promise*, he thought. *Looks like wesa winning after all.*

The Sith Lord attacked Obi-Wan relentlessly, backing him around the melting pit. All Obi-Wan's efforts could not break through his guard. And Obi-Wan was tiring, while his opponent seemed as fresh as ever.

Halfway around the melting pit, Obi-Wan dodged a vicious swing. The Sith Lord was on him before he could recover his balance. With a mighty stroke, the Sith knocked the young Jedi into the melting pit.

Time seemed to slow. Obi-Wan could hear the voices of his teachers in his memory: Qui-Gon saying over and over, *Trust the living Force, my young Padawan*, and Master Yoda, long ago, commanding, *Do, or do not. There is no try*. And now, for this moment, he understood. As he twisted to grab one of the input nozzles on the side of the pit, he thought dreamily, *That's what I have been doing wrong. I've been trying.*

On the walkway, the Sith Lord looked down at him, grinning evilly. With deliberate malice, he kicked Obi-Wan's lightsaber into the melting pit and watched it fall. Then he raised his lightsaber for the kill.

At the last minute, Obi-Wan flipped himself back up onto the walkway. Using the Force, he called Qui-Gon's lightsaber to him. The weapon slapped into his hand as he landed. The unexpected move caught the Sith Lord off guard. Smoothly, without trying, resting in the living Force, Obi-Wan swung his Master's lightsaber. The Sith Lord tried to parry, but he could not get his weapon around in time. He screamed and fell into the melting pit. Obi-Wan felt the tremor in the Force as he died.

Turning off the lightsaber, Obi-Wan ran back to Qui-Gon. "Master!"

"It is too late," Qui-Gon said in a voice filled with pain. "It's —"

"No!"

"Obi-Wan, promise —" Qui-Gon fought to get the words out. Obi-Wan could feel the effort he was making not to give in to the call of the Force. "Promise me you'll train the boy."

"Yes, Master."

Qui-Gon's face had a gray undertone, and his voice was growing fainter. Someone outside was cheering, and Obi-Wan had to lean closer to hear what his Master was saying. "He is the chosen one," Qui-Gon said. "He will . . . bring balance . . ." He gasped. "Train him!"

As the distant sounds of celebration grew louder, Obi-Wan felt the last breath leave Qui-Gon's body. He wanted to deny it, to refuse to believe, so that he could pretend to have even one more moment with the man who had been the only father he had ever known, but he could not. Weeping quietly, Obi-Wan knelt beside his dead Master, while outside the citizens of Naboo rejoiced in their sudden victory.

# CHAPTER 23

The following day, word came that the new Supreme Chancellor of the Galactic Republic would be arriving soon. *Better late than never,* Queen Amidala thought, although she had to admit that she would have been glad indeed to see him if her plans had failed.

The cruiser landed in the courtyard in front of the main hangar. Amidala had her troops bring the two Neimoidians, Nute Gunray and Rune Haako, to meet the ship. As they waited for the entrance ramp to be lowered, she turned to Gunray and said, "Now, Viceroy, you are going to have to go back to the Senate and explain all this."

"I think you can kiss your trade franchise goodbye," Captain Panaka added with considerable satisfaction.

The ramp opened at last. Obi-Wan and Panaka led the Neimoidians toward the ship as the new arrivals disembarked. First came Supreme Chancellor Palpatine, followed by several Republic guards. After them, a number of beings in Jedi robes came down the ramp. Obi-Wan stopped to talk to them.

Amidala moved forward to greet Palpatine. "Congratulations on your election, Chancellor," she said warmly. "It is so good to see you again."

"It is good to be home," Chancellor Palpatine said, smiling. "But it is you who should be congratulated. Your boldness has saved our people."

*But many died*, Amidala thought sadly. *Many of my people, and many Gungans. And Qui-Gon Jinn.* That news had hurt more than she would have believed possible.

"Tomorrow, we will celebrate our victory," she told the Chancellor. "Tonight . . . tonight we will grieve for those who are no longer here to celebrate."

The afternoon was a busy one. Obi-Wan spoke with Yoda and the other Jedi Masters, describing the battle with the Sith Lord in detail. When he finished, Mace Windu frowned. "There is no doubt. The mysterious warrior was a Sith."

"Always two there are," Master Yoda said pensively. "No more, no less. A master and an apprentice."

Master Windu nodded. "But which one was destroyed — the master, or the apprentice?"

No one had an answer. *But either way, there's still one of them out there,* Obi-Wan thought. *And if that was an apprentice, I hope I never have to face the master.*

When the discussion ended at last, Obi-Wan made his request — that once he passed the trials and became a full-fledged Jedi Knight, he be allowed to take Qui-Gon's place as Anakin Skywalker's Master. *I can never take his place, not really. But I can train Anakin.* The Masters looked thoughtful, and went off to confer in private. Late in the day, they summoned him again.

To Obi-Wan's surprise, only Master Yoda waited in the many-windowed room. He knelt and waited for the Jedi Master to speak. Master Yoda paced back and forth several times before turning to say abruptly, "Confer on you the level of Jedi Knight, the Council does." He frowned. "But agree with your taking this boy as your Padawan learner, I do not!"

"Qui-Gon believed in him," Obi-Wan said steadily. "I believe in Qui-Gon."

Yoda resumed his pacing. "The chosen one, the boy may be. Nevertheless, grave danger I fear in his training."

A shiver ran down Obi-Wan's spine, but he raised his head. "Master Yoda, I gave Qui-Gon my word. I *will* train Anakin. Without the approval of the Council, if I must."

"Qui-Gon's defiance I sense in you," Yoda said. "Need that, you do not!" He sighed. "Agree, the Council does. Your apprentice, young Skywalker will be."

Anakin stood staring at the funeral pyre. Everyone was here — Queen Amidala, Captain Panaka and his troops, Jar Jar and the Gungan leaders, Chancellor Palpatine, and the entire Jedi Council. Anakin looked around at them all, once, and then his eyes came back to the pyre where Qui-Gon's body burned. *He told me that if I stayed near him, I would be safe.* He sniffed, and rubbed the back of his hand against his nose. *I've lost everybody — Mom, Padmé, all my friends at home, and now Qui-Gon.*

Hands touched his shoulders, and he looked up. Obi-Wan looked gravely down at him. "He is one with the Force, Anakin," the Jedi said. "You must let go."

"What will happen to me now?" Anakin asked. Even to himself, he sounded forlorn.

"I am your Master now," Obi-Wan said solemnly.

Anakin looked up, startled. *Master? Not just guardian?* He felt hope rising. *I get to be a Jedi after all?*

As if he could read Anakin's thoughts, Obi-Wan smiled and nodded. "You will become a Jedi. I promise."

Comforted, Anakin stared into the flames. *I'll work hard to become a great Jedi,* he swore silently to Qui-Gon as the sparks of the funeral pyre rose into the night sky. *I'll make you proud of me.*

*I'll make you both proud.*

**PATRICIA C. WREDE** is one of today's most clever, inventive, and popular writers of fantasy. Her Enchanted Forest Chronicles — *Dealing with Dragons, Searching for Dragons, Calling on Dragons,* and *Talking to Dragons* — are among the most acclaimed (and best selling) YA fantasy novels of the decade. She is also the author of *Book of Enchantments, Mairelon the Magician,* and *Shadows over Lyra,* among others.

Before *The Phantom Menace*,
there was

# JEDI APPRENTICE

the story of young
Obi-Wan Kenobi and Qui-Gon Jinn

## CHAPTER 1

The blade of the lightsaber hissed through the air. Obi-Wan Kenobi could not see its red gleam through the blindfold pressing on his eyes. He used the Force to know precisely when to duck.

The searing heat of his opponent's lightsaber blade slashed overhead, nearly burning him. The air smelled like lightning.

"Good!" Yoda called from the sidelines of the room. "Let go. Let your feelings guide you."

The words of encouragement spurred Obi-Wan on. Because he was tall and strong for a twelve-year-old, many assumed that he'd have the advantage in battle.

But strength and size counted for nothing where agility and speed were needed. Nor did they have any effect on the Force that he had not yet mastered.

Obi-Wan listened intently for the sound of his

foe's lightsaber, for his breathing, for the scrape of a shoe against the floor. Such sounds echoed loudly in the small, high-ceilinged chamber.

A random jumble of blocks on the floor added another element to the exercise. He had to use the Force to sense those, too. With such uneven ground, it was easy to lose his footing.

Behind Obi-Wan, Yoda warned, "Keep your guard up."

Obi-Wan obediently raised his weapon and rolled to his right as his opponent's blade slammed down into the floor beside him. He took a small leap back, clearing a pile of blocks. Obi-Wan heard the sing of the lightsaber as his foe attempted a hasty strike motivated by irritation and fatigue. Good.

Sweat trickled underneath the blindfold, making his eyes sting. Obi-Wan blocked it out, along with his pleasure at his opponent's clumsiness. He could imagine himself a full Jedi Knight, battling a space pirate . . . a Togorian with fangs as long as Obi-Wan's fingers. In his mind, Obi-Wan saw the armored creature glare at him through eyes that were mere green slits. Its claws could easily shred a Human.

The vision energized him, helped him let go of his fears. In seconds, his every muscle was tuned to the Force. It moved through him, giving him the agility and speed that he needed.

Obi-Wan swung his blade up to block the next blow. The attacker's lightsaber hummed and whirled down. Obi-Wan leaped high, somersaulting over his attacker's head, and thrust his lightsaber down where the Togorian's heart would be.

"Aargh!" The other student howled in surprised rage as Obi-Wan's hot blade struck his neck. If Obi-Wan had been using a Jedi Knight's lightsaber, it would have been a killing blow. But apprentices in the Jedi Temple used training sabers set at low power. The touch of the blade only gave a searing kiss, one that the healers might need to tend.

"That was a lucky blow!" the wounded apprentice shouted.

Until that moment, Obi-Wan had not known who he was fighting. He'd been led into the room blindfolded. Now he recognized the voice: Bruck Chun. Like Obi-Wan, Bruck was one of the oldest apprentices in the Jedi Temple. Like Obi-Wan, Bruck hoped to be a Jedi Knight.

"Bruck," Yoda called calmly. "Leave your blindfold on. A Jedi needs not his eyes to see."

But Obi-Wan heard the boy's blindfold slap to the ground. Bruck's voice was choked with fury. "You clumsy oaf!"

"Calm yourself, you will!" Yoda warned Bruck in a sharp tone he rarely used.

Every student at the Jedi Temple had his or her weaknesses. Obi-Wan knew his own too well. Every day, he had to struggle to control his anger and his fear. The Temple was a test of character as much as skill.

Bruck struggled with his own simmering anger that could quickly ignite into hot rage. He usually kept it well under control, so that only other initiates had glimpsed it.

Bruck also held grudges. A year ago, Obi-Wan had stumbled in a Temple corridor, tripping Bruck, who had fallen. It had been an accident, caused by legs and feet that were growing too fast on both boys, but Bruck felt sure that Obi-Wan had done it on purpose. Bruck's dignity was very important to him. The laughter of the other students had goaded him. He'd called Obi-Wan an oaf then — *Oafy*-Wan.

The name had stuck.

The worst thing was that it was true. Often, Obi-Wan felt that his body was growing too fast. He couldn't seem to catch up with his long legs and large feet. A Jedi should feel comfortable in his body, but Obi-Wan felt awkward. Only when the Force was moving through him did he feel graceful or sure.

"Come on, Oafy," Bruck taunted. "See if you can hit me again! One last time, before they throw you out of the Temple!"

"Enough of that, Bruck!" Yoda said. "Learn to lose as well as win, a Jedi must. Go to your room, you will."

Obi-Wan tried not to feel the sting of Bruck's words. In four weeks he'd turn thirteen and would have to leave the Temple. Taunts like Bruck's were becoming more and more frequent as his birthday drew nearer. If he did not become a Padawan within the next four weeks, he'd be too old. He'd been listening for rumors intently, and had found that no Jedi was scheduled to come in search of a Padawan before it was too late. He was afraid that he'd never become a Jedi Knight. That fear angered him. Enough to make a foolish boast.

"You don't have to send him away, Master Yoda," he said. "I'm not afraid to fight *him* without his blindfold."

Color blazed in Bruck's cheeks, and his ice-blue eyes narrowed. Yoda merely nodded, taking in Obi-Wan's words. The truth was that Obi-Wan was just as exhausted as Bruck. He hoped Yoda would send both of them to their rooms instead of fighting again.

After a long moment, however, Yoda said, "All right. Continue. Much to learn, you have. Use the blindfolds, you must."

Obi-Wan turned and bowed to Yoda, accepting the order. He knew that Yoda was fully aware of his fatigue. Although he wished that the Master would grant him a reprieve, he accepted the wisdom of all of Yoda's decisions, great and small.

Obi-Wan tightened his blindfold. He pushed away his fatigue, willed his muscles to obey. He tried to forget that he was fighting Bruck, or that his chance to become a Jedi Knight was almost past. He concentrated instead on the image of the Togorian pirate, its orange-striped fur covered by black armor.

Obi-Wan could sense the Force flowing around him, within him. He could feel the living Force in Bruck, the dark ripples caused by Bruck's anger. His impulse was to match that anger with his own. He had to resist it.

Obi-Wan assumed a defensive stance as Bruck lunged. He let the Force guide him, as it had done earlier. He blocked the next blow easily. Then he jumped high to avoid another blow and landed behind a pillar. Lightsabers smashed together, sputtered and burned, then whisked apart. The air felt thicker, clogged with the energy of the battle.

For long minutes, the two students fought as if in a graceful dance. Obi-Wan leaped away from every attack and blocked every jarring blow. He did not try to hit Bruck.

*Let him see that I'm not clumsy,* Obi-Wan

thought bitterly. *Let him see that I'm not stupid. Let him see it over and over again.*

Sweat began to drench Obi-Wan's clothes. His muscles burned. He could hardly breathe fast enough to get the air he needed. But as long as he did not attack in anger, the Force remained strong with him. He tried not to think about the fight. He lost himself in the dance, and soon he felt so weary, he did not think at all.

Bruck fought slower and slower. Soon, Obi-Wan did not even need to leap away from Bruck's weary attacks. He merely blocked them, until finally Bruck gave up.

"Good, Obi-Wan," Yoda called. "Learning you are."

Obi-Wan switched off his lightsaber and hung it on his belt. He used the blindfold to wipe the sweat from his face. Next to him, Bruck was doubled over, panting. He did not look at Obi-Wan.

"You see," Yoda said. "To defeat an enemy, you do not have to kill. Defeat the rage that burns in him, and he is your enemy no longer. Rage the true enemy is."

Obi-Wan understood what Yoda meant. But Bruck's glazed glare told Obi-Wan that he had not defeated his opponent's anger. Nor had he won the boy's respect.

The two boys turned to Yoda and bowed

solemnly. A vision of his friend Bant rose in Obi-Wan's head. One of the best things about beating Bruck would be telling her about it.

"Enough for one day," Yoda said. "Tomorrow, a Jedi Knight comes to the Temple seeking a Padawan. Ready for him you must be."

Obi-Wan tried to hide his surprise. Usually, when a Knight came to the Temple in search of a Padawan, rumors beat the arrival by days. That way, if a student wanted to earn the honor of becoming the Knight's Padawan, he or she could prepare mentally and physically.

"Who?" Obi-Wan asked, heart racing. "Who's coming?"

"Seen him before, you have," Yoda said. "Master Qui-Gon Jinn."

# Meet the Guardians of the Force.

# STAR WARS®

## JEDI APPRENTICE

The young Obi-Wan Kenobi.
The great Jedi Master,
Qui-Gon Jinn.

Experience their adventures across
the galaxy.

Read the all-new
Jedi Apprentice Series.

**Jedi Apprentice #1: The Rising Force**
by Dave Wolverton

**Jedi Apprentice #2: The Dark Rival**
by Jude Watson

Coming to bookstores this May.

SWJA1198